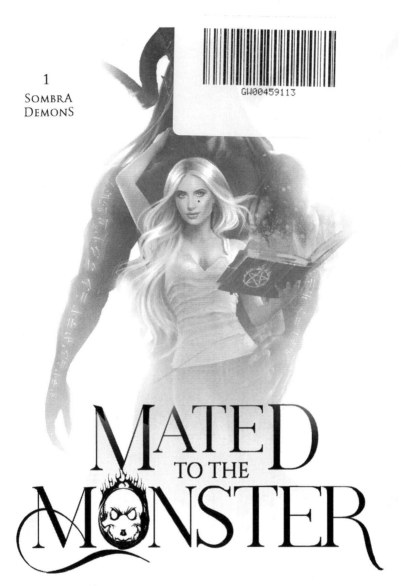

1

SOMBRA
DEMONS

MATED
TO THE
MONSTER

INTERNATIONAL BESTSELLING AUTHOR
SARAH SPADE

Cover by Claire Holt of Luminescence Covers

Exclusive illustration by S.J. Fowler of Night Witchery

FOREWORD

Thank you for checking out *Mated to the Monster*!

This is a steamy monster romance (intended for 18+) with explicit scenes and some profanity. It's the love story between Shannon, a human woman, and Malphas, a Sombra demon. He has two forms: a demonic form (illustrated on the hardback cover) and the shadowy shape (illustrated on the eBook/paperback's cover), both with demon traits like a bulky size, fangs, and horns. It relies heavily on the fated mates trope, as well as instalove—at least on Mal's part. For Shannon, she at least makes it a week before she realizes that she's meant to be mated to her monster.

It's also the beginning of a series of standalones with each eventual story featuring a different couple.

I hope you enjoy!

xoxo,
Sarah

CHAPTER 1
YELLOW CHALK

SHANNON

It takes me three stores to find colored chalk.

The fact that I kept looking instead of pulling my phone out and placing an order for a pack is all anyone needs to know to figure out how I tick. Once I set my mind on something, I have no *off* switch. There is no *wait*. I make decisions—sometimes recklessly so—and I never second-guess them. I'll keep going and going until I accomplish what I set out to do, or something else stops me first.

Or I get bored.

Or distracted.

Tori says I'm impulsive. She's not wrong. Still, I can also be pretty single-minded when I want to. Like now. I've had this old-fashioned, leather-bound book for a couple of weeks, ever since I bought it on a whim from the used bookstore a couple of blocks away from my apartment. To be honest, I totally forgot about it until last night after work when I was searching my closet for something else. I saw the bag I tossed in there all those weeks ago, remembered Kennedy selling me the book, then figured it might be worth it to see what was inside of it.

I knew it was a spellbook. I mean, it has a pentacle —an inverted star whose five points touch the circle surrounding it—embossed on the cover. There's no title on the front, no author, either, though the cover page simply says: *Grimoire du Sombra*, whatever that means.

When I opened it up last night, choosing a page at random, I was delighted to see that it was a true love spell. Like, really? I thought Kennedy was pulling my leg when she said it was a spellbook, but I was charmed enough by its uniqueness that I bought it anyway.

But a love spell?

Heck, *yeah*, I was gonna try that out.

Of course, that led me to the chalk conundrum. Before attempting the spell, there were instructions on what I had to do, and when one of them was to draw a protective symbol with a piece of yellow chalk, I had to hold off until this morning when I could find some. I had everything else I would need—an open space, a clear floor, cooking salt, and a willingness to be loved… seriously, that's what it said—except for the chalk.

But now I have it. Score one for Shannon!

It's mid-afternoon by the time I return to my apartment with my shopping bag. As eager as I am to amuse myself with an attempt at "spell-casting", I toss the bag of chalk next to the book and the container of salt already on top of my messy, unmade bed, then go to the kitchen to throw together a quick lunch.

Hey. Girl's gotta eat. Can't summon your true love on an empty stomach, you know?

Once I've dropped all of my dishes into my sink, I throw my hair up into a ponytail, roll my sleeves back, then rub my hands together. Snorting to myself, I think, "Time to do some magic," then go and grab the spellbook.

It's old. Like, *really* old. The pages are super thin and yellowed, and they have that musty old book smell that makes me want to curl up on my couch and read into the night.

Maybe after I check out this spell and laugh about how ridiculous I was for even trying, I'll flip through the rest of it just for shits and giggles. So far, I've only paid attention to the one page—the one spell—and now that I have my chalk, I flip right to it.

At the top of the page, the words **VERUS AMOR** are printed in a heavy block typeface. Someone has scrawled *true love* beneath it in a delicate script that takes me longer than I'll ever admit to make out. Luckily, the rest of the handwritten comments decorating the margins are in a legible print.

The previous owner of this book must've taken the spells seriously. I figure, why not, and decide to do the same. If they say to use yellow chalk to draw the protective symbol, then pour salt in a circle around that, I don't see the harm in following the instructions precisely.

Besides, it's not like it's going to work or anything…

It's the weekend. Saturday to be exact. I don't go back to the office until Monday, and I didn't have any plans except for my daily trip to The Beanery where I get my caffeine mix and moon over Derek whenever he's on shift. One of these days I might work up the nerve to let the barista know I'm into him, but since that's not today, why shouldn't I mess around with an old book of spells?

Way I see it, jokingly casting a love spell can't hurt. Either I end up with the love of my life—maybe I'll get lucky and it'll turn out to be the swoon-worthy Derek—or I have a ridiculous story to tell my co-workers on Monday.

So, the first thing I need is a piece of yellow chalk. Grabbing the bag from the dollar store, I rip open the small box of chalk I managed to find after walking around all of Jericho this morning; my neighborhood is a suburb of a big city, so while I have a car, I usually prefer to walk down our pretty stacked Main Street. Makes it a little harder to find small necessities like chalk, but when there's a will, there's a way, and now I have five different colors in a pack of ten.

Rifling through the box, I see pink, blue, green—*ah*.

"Yellow chalk, check. Let's go."

With the symbol drawn in the margin as a guide, I kick aside my throw rug and use the chalk to draw another pentacle on the hardwood floor in my bedroom. There are a couple of sigils that go around the points of the star. It takes me a good ten minutes to copy them. I only hope I did that right.

That done, I reach for the salt. The instructions say, for added protection, I should go around the drawing twice so that the circle is complete. I'm not really sure why I need protection when the point of this spell is to manifest my true love to me, but I do it anyway. In fact, I use every last bit of salt in the container, just in case, then toss the empty.

What's next?

Wiping the chalk dust and stray granules against my jeans, I peer down at the page. The old owner had drawn a bracket around one part of the printed page, then a second around a paragraph at the bottom. They also wrote *manifest* near the first part, and *promise* plus a star next to the second paragraph.

Okay, then.

It's not in English. The printed part, I mean. Like

the title of the spell at the top, it's in a weird language I don't understand; unlike the title, there is no translation. I typed a couple of words into my phone last night to see what they said, but apart from a few of them flagging as Latin, some as French, others as Portuguese, it doesn't make any real sense.

Then again, it's a spell. Is it supposed to? For all I know, the mysterious author took a mishmash of foreign words, added them to some they made up themselves, and passed it along as a "grimoire" for gullible schmucks like me.

The downside to this not being any real language is I have no freaking clue how to pronounce the words. So, hoping for the best, I give it the old college try, grateful that I live alone.

If I was back home with my parents, or I had a roommate like I did in my early twenties, I would never live this down. Of course, they'd expect something like this from me, but I'd still be razzed until the end of time.

The spell's a mouthful. I stumble over the words, only committing to the bit because I went so far as to find the yellow chalk in the first place. This, I decide, is what happens when you have a three-year celibacy streak. You resort to pretending you can cast a true love spell in the sanctity of your messy bedroom.

Only… I don't think it's pretend.

I can't believe it. I really freaking can't. If it wasn't for me seeing it with my own two eyes, I'd call bullshit, but tell that to the sparking sound and plume of smoke that suddenly appears in the middle of my chalk drawing as soon as I finish saying the last word in the first section of the spell.

Something… uh, something's happening.

Welp. That can't be good.

Slamming the book closed, I toss it on the bed behind me in case I need both of my hands. I don't know why I would, but when the smoke starts to darken, then widens before revealing a split in the air, I should probably be prepared to defend myself.

And, yes, that certainty lasts for maybe twenty seconds. After that, I'm completely paralyzed as I watch the split turn into an opening about as big as a hula hoop.

Hot air rushes out of it. Like, open a roasting oven set to 450 degrees and get a face full of dry heat *hot*. It slams into me, even a few feet away, and I have to squint to look past it.

I gasp. Can't move, but I choke on my next breath.

Is that Hell? It… it looks like what I imagine Hell might. The sky is dark. Shadowed. A bright red sun— or maybe moon—hangs low in the distance, a beacon that immediately draws my attention. Its illumination reveals a ground made of black-and-grey ash, with bleached white skulls bathed in red dotting the landscape.

The skulls… they all have horns.

"What… what the—"

A patch of the sky falls to the ground. At least, that's what I thought until I notice that it's a dark, shadowy figure arrowing toward me—and the hole that's still wide open.

The realization that I actually created some kind of portal *and* that I might have accidentally invited this shadow thing to come into my room is enough to break my momentary spell of paralysis. I jump away from the salt circle as if that's going to stop that shadow from rushing closer.

It doesn't, but there's got to be some way to shut this portal.

Only… *how*?

The spellbook, my panicked mind screams at me. I need the book.

Where did I put that stupid thing?

My bed! That's right, I left it on my bed. Without taking my eyes off of the portal to Hell, I back up against the mattress, groping wildly with my left hand. I get a fistful of blanket, fingers scrabbling against my sheet before I finally hit the pitted leather cover.

Yes!

I grab the book, quickly flipping to the page I marked with a receipt from The Beanery. I drag my trembling finger down until I hit the last line I read. I go to the paragraph printed beneath it, the one with the big star drawn in pen right next to it.

It's gotta be important. A way to close the portal perhaps?

I really hope so.

It's written in the same language. I stumble over the first two words, but before I can read the rest, I realize I'm too late.

The mass of shadows has slipped right through the portal.

Crossing from that hellish dimension into my bedroom, it stops as soon as the last vestiges of the shadow makes it through. The portal immediately winks out behind it, leaving the black shadows in the center of the circle of salt, hovering directly over my chalk drawing of the pentacle.

My jaw drops.

CHAPTER 2
SURVIVAL INSTINCTS

SHANNON

As I watch in a mixture of fear and morbid curiosity, the shadows actually take on a shape. Still mostly amorphous, there's no denying the sharp horns jutting out of the head, or the hulking body that forms next. Eyes appear about two feet higher than mine; they're a glowing golden color that seem like a pair of headlights shining out of a dark face framed with flowing, shoulder-length black hair. Weirdo characters form along the side of the shape—its arms, maybe—and they have the same glow as its eyes.

The whole shadow monster is like something out of my worst nightmares. I'm too scared to scream, to *move*, and I can't do anything but watch as it continues to form. The more I stare with my mouth hanging open, the more I can pick out other features—and *monster* is right. It has fangs. When it opens its mouth, forming a break in its shadowy lips, I see gleaming white fangs, and thick fingers that end in pointed claws.

And that's not all.

Right at the juncture of its legs, forming under my shameless gaze, is a shadowy dick that looks like a freaking *club*. It fits the monster's size, but that doesn't mean it isn't the most terrifying—and, honestly, impressive—cock I've ever seen.

It—no, *he*—he isn't done transforming. The shadows settle against my meticulously drawn chalk lines before his feet become solid. As soon as they do, the rest of him instantly changes. Instead of a floating shadowy shape, he is a seven-foot-tall horned monster with black hair, golden eyes, dark red skin, and muscles bigger than my head.

Holy fucking shit.

I blink. Mostly because I can't believe what I'm seeing, and I really, really hope that this is a figment of my imagination brought on by reading that silly, old spellbook, but also because what else can you do when faced with a demon who looks like he's straight out of Hell?

And I brought him here.

He opens his mouth, revealing his inch-long fangs again. I choke on a gasp as he says something in a language that sounds strangely like the spell I was fooling around with. I have no clue what the harsh syllables he says mean, but he's not snarling, and he's not attacking me.

No. He's actually holding his hand out toward me as though he wants me to come to him.

Oh, *heck* no.

Nope. Nope nope nope. No way am I going over there. I only hope that the circle of salt does its job and keeps him trapped on top of the pentacle I drew because I'm not going anywhere near a towering monster from Hell.

Uh-uh.

Especially not a *naked* one.

I can't help it. I don't know what else it says about me that, while avoiding his outstretched hand, I glance down again. It's as if my eyes have a lusty, pervy mind of their own. I could've looked anywhere else around the room, but I didn't, and that's when I see that his second form doesn't have a stitch of clothing on it—and that his huge cock is even bigger when it's erect.

Because it is. It totally is.

"Oh my god," I breathe out. "I… holy shit. Are you fucking kidding me?"

He answers me in his language. What does he say? No clue. I barely make out the sharp syllables in his deep, guttural voice as I stare in horror at his junk. Where the rest of him is a deep blood-red color, his shaft has turned dark purple as it stiffened. There's no missing that sucker, or what it implies.

This monster from Hell is down to fuck, and I'm obviously the only chick here—and the one who fooled around with a spellbook in order to summon my true love…

No. It can't be. Maybe… maybe traveling from his dimension has a side effect. Could be, right? Go from Hell to Earth and get a hard-on, that's all.

He's not my true love. He's not even *human*.

My head shoots up to look at his face. To be fair, his features are somewhat human-*ish*. I mean, he has two eyes, a normal nose, lush lips that hide his fangs when they're pressed together, and a set of pointed ears that peek out beneath his mess of silky black hair. If it weren't for the bumps over his nose and the gleaming onyx horns jutting from his brow—and, you know, the red skin—he might be an oversized man.

But he's not.

"Uxor," he rasps out. With a fist that's bigger than a freaking softball, he pounds his muscular chest, then points at me. A look of absolute hunger flashes across his face as he says, "Uxor mi."

The claw on the tip of his finger is at least two inches long.

Uxor mi… I have no idea what that means. But between the way he's pointing at me, the swivel of his hips as though he wants to make sure I can't miss his cock—as if I *could*—and the worrying way *mi* sounds way too much like *me*… yeah.

I take one step away from him, then another.

The monster frowns, then says something else. He rattles off more syllables than I can catch, though I'm not really listening. Right now, my only focus is on getting the heck out of Dodge before he figures out how to get out of the circle.

Because he will. If he can, he will. And after I saw that look of hunger on the demon's face, I'm not sure what he'll do, but one thing for sure?

I'm not about to stick around and find out.

I RAN.

I'm not ashamed to admit it. Show me someone who says they wouldn't bolt for their door if a shadow monster materializes in the middle of their bedroom like that, and I'll show you someone who is full of shit. It was pure survival instinct. With the creature's dark shape, his fiery eyes, and the glowing squiggles decorating his side, I didn't know what it was or where it came from—and that was before he solidified into a hulking demon with horns, blood-red skin, and his massive dick swinging between his thick thighs before going hard.

After that, I had to go. If only to put some space between me and the demon I accidentally summoned,

I had to get away from him so I could figure out what to do next.

So I bolted for my front door, not caring in the least that I was leaving the monster alone in my apartment. I didn't stop when I emerged into the hallway, either. Still clutching the spellbook, I tore down the hall, using my shoulder to throw open the door that led to the staircase. My apartment is on the fourth floor, and I scurried down all three flights while panting, "Holy shit, holy *shit*," under my breath.

The lobby is usually empty this time of day. My neighbors are either unwinding from work, getting ready to go out for the weekend, or having dinner. In case it's not, I force myself to stop halfway down the final flight, squeezing the spellbook until the shock isn't so overwhelming.

Okay. I have a huge demonic creature *thing* in my apartment—in my freaking *bedroom*—and no idea what I'm supposed to do now. I don't even know if he'll be there when I get back. Will the circle hold him? Maybe I'll get lucky and the portal will reopen, he'll cross back over, and this will be one of those things I take with me to my grave.

Heck, if this all turns out to be a figment of my imagination, that would be totally fine, too. Because a naked male monster who reached for me as his club of a cock came to life? Yeah, *no*. I still don't have any idea what to do about that.

But *Kennedy* might.

It's a long shot. Taking a deep breath, using a shaky hand to shove a stray strand of hair out of my face, I push through the door that leads to the lobby. The way I see it, if Kennedy sold me the book, maybe she can help. At the very least, she might be able to tell me where she got it from since it's the only one of its kind.

I know that for a fact, too. When she convinced me it was worth the fifty bucks she asked for it because it was so rare, I checked Amazon to make sure she wasn't ripping me off. Then, when I couldn't find it there or on eBay, I forked over the money because— say it with me now—Shannon is recklessly impulsive.

And, boy, am I regretting that now.

Even more when I speed walk the six blocks from my apartment building and discover all of the lights inside of Turn the Page are off.

Kennedy owns and runs the used bookstore all on her own. She's a staff of one, and she's there seven days a week, from open to close. Foot traffic winds down on Main Street around sunset as most shops close around that time, but it's barely mid-afternoon. The store shouldn't be closed.

Yet it is.

That's on me. With everything going on, I forgot that Kennedy was going on vacation. It even says that right on the note she has posted on the inside of her door. Turn the Page is closed through the end of next week.

Of course it is.

The disappointment slams into me like a Mack truck. My adrenaline seeps out as my energy flags. Crap. What now?

Without even giving my tired legs the order, I find myself heading inside of The Beanery. The enticing aroma of pastries and freshly brewed coffee brings me around a little, and I approach the counter because it seems like the best thing to do.

Derek is still here. That's a little surprising. I don't want to consider myself a stalker or anything, but I've kind of picked up on his schedule lately. He's usually gone home by this time on a Saturday.

Normally I'd be happy to see him. I've been into him for a couple of months now, though he doesn't seem to have a clue. True, my flirting skills are a little rusty, and something about the barista with the curly brown hair and deep brown eyes gets me a little tongue-tied, but I would've thought it was obvious by this point. And maybe it is. Maybe he's not interested in me. Sucks, but whatever.

At the very least, he's never acted anything other than your friendly, neighborhood coffee guy. For once, that comes in handy as he calls out a greeting to me. I know friendly Derek. Friendly Derek is normal. Ordinary. Coffee is good.

I can do this.

"How are you?"

MATED TO THE MONSTER

"Good, good," he answers. "So, what can I get for you, Shannon? The usual?"

"Um. Yeah. Sure."

He punches my order into his register, then turns to start making it. As he does, Derek shifts back to look at me again. His brow furrows. "Hey. You okay?"

Me? Oh, yeah. I only played around with a spellbook and now there's a big, red demon monster thing *in my apartment, but other than that, I'm peachy.*

I force my lips into a grin. "Doing great. How much do I owe you?"

"$4.50. Same as always."

Right. Because I get the same drink every day. I didn't even think to question it when Derek said "the usual" like that, even though I already got my morning coffee.

Shaking my head, I go to grab my purse… only to remember as Derek's finishing up steaming the milk for my latte that I ran out of the house with my spellbook and nothing else.

"*Crap.*"

"What's wrong?"

I sigh. Right now, it's all I *can* do. "You're not gonna believe this, but I totally spaced on bringing my purse. It's got my phone and my wallet in it, and I walked over without it."

Derek snaps the lid on my latte to-go cup. "Don't worry about it. Accidents happen. Get me tomorrow, alright?"

Because we both know that I'll be back.

Unless, you know, I return to my apartment and the shadow monster I left behind is waiting to gobble me up.

"Really?" I ask, shoving that idea out of my over-imaginative brain. "You sure?"

He slides the cup toward me. "Of course. Besides, seems like you might need this."

He has no freaking idea.

CHAPTER 3
NOSY NEIGHBORS

SHANNON

I drink my entire latte—no. Wait. Not true. First, I guzzle a couple of sips, cursing a blue streak when I burn the crap out of my tongue, then let it cool. After it has, I do drink my entire latte, praying the caffeine will help me come up with my next brilliant idea.

Should've remembered that two lattes in one day is one past my limit. I've barely finished this one when I start to feel anxious and wired. Not the best thing considering what I have waiting for me at home.

It gets even worse when I decide: fuck it. I'm not going to let the monster run me out of my apartment. At this point, let him try to eat me. It's gotta be better than walking down Main Street with no money, no phone, and my hands shaking in a combination of caffeine and nerves.

On the plus side, I don't run into anyone on my way back up to the fourth floor. Even better, there's no seven-foot-tall monster waiting on the other side of the door to attack me. He's still standing right where I left him. Still imposing. Still naked. Not quite so hard, though that immediately starts to change when he sees me poking my head around the doorway leading to my room.

I'm caught. No doubt about that. I decide to own it, if only because his staying on the chalk drawing after my escape means that he probably has to for some reason.

He says something. The only word I pick up is *uxor*, probably because he used it on me before.

I hold up my hand as I cross over to him.

He tilts his horns toward me, but he stops talking.

Here goes nothing. Running didn't work, and I can't just pretend that I don't have a massive demonic creature in the middle of my bedroom. One way or another, we have to talk.

"Can you... do you understand me?"

The demon watches me closely. He stays silent.

Crap. I'm going to take that as a *no* then. I still try to find a way to communicate with him if only because it makes me feel a little better about this whole thing.

How about some charades?

"Can you"—I point at his chest—"step out of the circle"—gesturing at the salt, I mime an oversized step with my right foot—"and come out here"—I point to the ground— "with me?"

In retrospect, I probably shouldn't have jabbed my boob to indicate *me*, especially when his high-beams turn on even brighter as I basically grope myself.

Men. Doesn't matter if they're demons or humans, they're still the same.

I clear my throat, dragging his attention back to my face. "Well?" I go through the motions again with the exception of poking my boob. Waving at my body seems to make him as… um… *happy*, but I think he finally gets the message this time when I say, "Can you?"

With a solemn nod of understanding, he makes a move toward me.

I immediately regret asking him. Did I just give him permission to leave the circle?

I… I don't think so.

As though he slammed into a glass wall, he stops short—but that's not all. Once he reaches the inner edge of the circle of salt, something sizzles, the bitter scent of paper burning fills the room, and the monster goes up in smoke.

No. Not smoke. *Shadow.* He turns into the same shadowy figure with glowing golden eyes and rune-like characters running up and down the length of his beefy arms.

Doesn't matter that I've seen that form before. I still shriek in surprise at how quickly all that happened.

Too late do I realize how freaking loud my shriek was. I slap my hand over my mouth, but the damage is already done.

Right as the monster's shadowy form begins to change back to the solid, red-skinned demon I'd grown used to, I hear a knock at my door, followed by a familiar voice.

"Shannon? Are you in there? I saw you run out before. Now I thought I heard a scream. Are you alright?"

Mrs. Winslow.

Crap.

Turning back to the well-hung monster, I purposely meet his glowing gaze. "Stay here, okay?"

Like he can go anywhere else. His little display proved that he's stuck inside of the circle. Score another point for yellow chalk and salt!

"Just… be quiet." I lift my hand to my lips, hushing him. My nosy neighbor obviously noticed my freak-out earlier. How will I ever be able to explain *this*? "I'll be right back."

He doesn't know English the same way I can't understand his harsh language, but wherever the hell he's from—and something tells me that *Hell* really isn't too far off there—our gestures must mean the same thing. Either that or he's mocking me because he folds his massive fist before extending his pointer finger. He slaps it against his mouth and nods.

Good enough.

Shutting my bedroom door behind me, I dash for the entrance to my apartment. A quick peek through the peephole reveals a middle-aged woman with a friendly smile and a pair of shrewd dark eyes.

Mrs. Winslow is the type of neighbor who will wish you good morning when you cross paths in the hall, then call the landlord on you if you so much as put your television's volume at an "unacceptable" level. Since I've lived here, I learned not to make an enemy of her, and if I refuse to answer her, how much do I bet that she'll start paying attention to what I'm doing?

Usually, I wouldn't give a shit. Then again, usually, I don't have a monster in my room.

My ponytail is listing to the side, hanging low after my earlier mad dash. I yank my ponytail holder out, sliding it onto my wrist, then quickly run my fingers through my hair. When I'm as presentable as I'm going to get on such short notice, I crack open my door.

My message is clear. I'm being a friendly neighbor, but my friendliness has its limits. I'll talk to Mrs. Winslow, but no way am I letting her inside for a chat.

"Hi. Sorry about that. The scream, I mean. You heard me?"

"I'm sure everyone in the building heard that,

dear." Her lips purse enough to show me she's not too happy with me, and not only because of the scream. She was probably banking on wrangling an invite. Oh, well. She pushes anyway. "Is everything okay?"

Just once, I'd love to say *no*. To admit what I did, and see if one of them wants to fix my mess for me.

But I don't. Instead, I smile. "It's fine. I thought I saw a mouse, but I realized that it was a big ol' dust bunny instead."

"If you kept your apartment swept and cleaned, dear, that wouldn't happen."

My smile wavers. "True enough. If you'll excuse me, I'll get right on that."

"Mmm. Did the same dust bunny chase you out into the hall before? The way you were running like that, I was so worried for you."

It's a little harder to hold onto my smile. "Thanks for your concern, but everything's okay here."

My tone is friendly, yet firm. Final. This conversation is over.

Mrs. Winslow understands. "Don't mention it, Shannon. You know I'm always just a few doors away."

"I know, Mrs. Winslow."

Believe me, I *know*. And I understand, too.

I can tell that she wants to say something else but, before she can, I waggle my fingers at her.

"Have a good night," I tell her, then quickly ease my front door closed again.

I wait a moment until I hear her footsteps heading down the hall. Once I do, I lock my door. Bracing my back against the wood, I tilt my head, closing my eyes as I realize that I didn't fool my neighbor one bit, I have a shadow monster I can't talk to in my bedroom, and still no clue how to fix any of this.

My go-to is out. Somehow, I don't think running to Google to see if someone else found themselves in this same sitch is going to work.

Then again… hey. It can't hurt.

Right?

DO YOU KNOW WHAT THE RESULTS SAY WHEN YOU google "how to banish a demon?" No? Well, now I do.

And it doesn't freaking work.

Did I really expect it to? Nah. But I was desperate, and when the second search result was literally a Wikihow article that explained a few steps on how to banish a demon, I tried. I didn't have any sage to burn, but I had some of the dried stuff in my spice cabinet. Clutching the container behind me in one hand, I tip-toed back into my bedroom.

The demon was still in his red-skinned, muscular, *solid* form. As soon as I reappeared in the doorway, his head shot up as he tried talking to me.

His voice had gone softer. Gentler. In that strange,

foreign language of his, he said something to me that almost sounds like he's trying to cajole me. I still couldn't understand a word of it, but I edged closer to him as if I could.

His eyes lit up. From the way his shoulders bounced, I bet he was trying to show his massive cock off to me again.

No, thanks.

As I moved slowly, super careful not to look below neck level, he frowned for a moment, then lifted up a hand that was more massive than a catcher's mitt, crooking a finger at me. At the end of his finger, he had a black claw that was so much longer than one of mine.

Because, you know, the fangs hanging past his bottom lip weren't bad enough.

Still, I sucked it the fuck up. I let him think that I'd gotten past being afraid up until I was about a foot away. Then, hoping it'll work, I hurriedly sprinkled the dried sage on him.

He sneezed with such force that his long black hair fell forward, barely hiding his snarl.

I squealed and dashed back out to my living room.

As soon as my heart stopped beating the samba in my chest, I go back to peeking my head around the doorway. His eyes were glowing like molten gold, but he didn't look as fierce as he had in the aftermath of his sneeze. That was a good thing. Considering the sage didn't do shit to banish him, it's probably a good thing I didn't piss him off.

So, sage was out. I'd been praying from the moment I realized I'd accidentally summoned a monster with an old spellbook so I skipped over step two. Step three said to bang a wooden spoon against one of my pans to scare any demons away.

I risked Mrs. Winslow coming by to check up on me again by hitting the spoon against the side of my favorite soup pot. Not only did it not work, but I discovered that the demon has a harsh grating laugh when I marched into my bedroom, closed the door, and banged the pot in front of him.

Step four was holy water. Yeah... if praying couldn't help, I doubted that would, though I was saving that as a last resort. I haven't set foot in a church in years and I could just imagine sneaking it, stealing some holy water, and having to explain myself when I inevitably got caught.

At that point, I started skim-reading the article, but when I got to the part that said I could keep demons away by watching the right movies and listening to positive music, I snorted and backed out of the page.

He tried to say something to me again, and I nodded, shot him a thumbs up, and cheerily told him to hold his horses, that I was working on getting him back to Hell as soon as possible.

Of course, he didn't understand. Good chance I

was wasting my breath, but I'd gone from terrified straight to determined, and if this was how I was going to deal with having a big red demon in my apartment, he'd have to deal, too.

When I see another result mentioning a banishing spell, I remember the spellbook, then feel like a freaking dope that I never thought to search its pages for some way to reverse the other spell. Why not, right? If the book made it so that I could bring him here, I should be able to send him back.

Still keeping him in my sight, I inch back over to my bed, snagging the spellbook I kept close by.

Last night, when I first opened up the grimoire, I found the true love spell and never searched past that. I was intrigued by the idea that a spell could bring me a man, and already entertained by the prospect of playing along. I gave up when I saw that I would need the yellow chalk, but I never looked at any of the other pages to see the different types of spells in the book.

I do now.

First, I flip through the yellowed pages, then I go more slowly. Plopping down on the edge of my bed, the demon copies me, sinking down to sit on top of my chalk drawing. He folds his legs beneath him, his bulk bowing over so that we're closer in height.

Whether he caught on to how I'm avoiding meeting his one-eyed monster or not, he tucks his dick out of sight, even as that hungry, determined expression of his stays locked on my face. I've seen enough guys looking at me and visualizing me naked to know that, despite our obvious… *differences*, he would have me flat on my back in a heartbeat if I gave him the "go" sign.

That realization spurs me to keep searching.

Too bad there's nothing for me to find. Unlike the true love spell, not a single other page is marked, either in pencil or pen—except for the inner cover.

I didn't notice it yesterday, but the mysterious owner has a name. Scrawled in the same script as the comments in the margins, she signed the inside of the front cover: *Susanna M. Benoit*. Directly beneath it, a child—considering the chicken scratch, it had to be a young child—had added three crooked letters: **AMY**.

And… that's all.

Because I'm reaching, I trade the spellbook for my phone and do a quick search for this Susanna, but—surprise, surprise—I come up empty.

Well, no. That's not exactly true. I find a handful of mentions of a Susanna M. Benoit from thirty years ago. Since it's a couple of newspaper articles about her sudden and unexpected disappearance all those years ago, that doesn't help me much, and I give up on following that lead.

Unfortunately, that leaves me at a dead end.

The spell doesn't work. Neither did the banishing from the Wikihow web article. The demon monster can't understand a word I'm saying, though he seems to be a whiz at charades.

Now if only I can explain to him that I have no idea what he's doing here, or how to get him back to where he came from.

How exactly am I supposed to mime *that*?

CHAPTER 4
SHANNON

MALPHAS

My mate is an odd creature.

Firstly, she's human. So maybe that's to be expected. I'm not sure.

You see, if I was surprised when a portal opened while I was bathing this eve, that's nothing compared to the shock I knew when I found myself trapped inside of a protective circle, looking down at my mate for the first time and discovering she is one of the fabled mortals spoken of in whispers by my clansmen.

She's so… so *tiny*, too.

At least two heads smaller than I am, and nearly half my bulk, she is a slender slip of a female. No horns, I notice, my first clue that she's not demonkind like I am. Her skin is pale and washed-out compared to my Sombran form. Long, silky hair falls down her back, so fair it's nearly white; already I imagine fisting the strands as I arch her back to take her lips in my claiming kiss. The only true color on her belongs to her eyes. As blue as the rare morning sky in Sombra, they're as lovely—and unique—as my mortal mate.

Even her fastenings are in dull shades: a white top hiding a bounty of breasts, and dark trousers that cover legs I ache to wrap around me. I've never mated before—Sombra demons get one true mate, and we wait for them for as long as it takes—but I've spent many a solitary night stroking my cock to the idea of the one female meant for me.

All my imaginings pale in comparison to my new reality.

My mate is beautiful, if unlike any female I've seen before, and my body stirs as she gapes in surprise at me. As shocked as I am to discover she's human, I know she would never expect to find her male in a Sombra demon. Probably because Duke Haures and his counterparts in the other realms have spent two thousand years ensuring that demonkind has been kept separate from this human world full of mortals.

And, yet, I'm here. This mortal is mine. I recognize it instinctively, as if a part of me has been missing my entire life, and I only now know what it was: this tiny fair-haired female. I never thought I would be so fortunate to find her at all, let alone such a stunning creature, and I take her in with a gaze so hungry, it's a miracle I'm not drooling in front of her.

An age ago, a clan seer foretold that my mate would bloom in the sun, and she'd be full of magic. I obviously took that to mean that she would be from Soleil, a neighboring plane with plenty of female demons who all have golden skin, orange hair, deep brown horns, and enough power to banish the shadows from any Sombra male.

Most of my kind find their mates in Soleil females. They are the perfect complement for us, and the world closest to ours. We either choose to follow our mate to Soleil, or bring her home with us to Sombra, but travel between demon planes is easy.

Traveling to the human realm is almost unheard of.

It's Duke Haures's first law. Our peoples are simply too different, and the ruler of Sombra refuses to allow his demons to cross into this world on their own. The only exception? When our mate summons us to their side.

Like mine did to me.

The moment her spell reached me through worlds, I knew that my long wait was finally at an end. Most males imprint upon their mate within their first few centuries. I've waited more than ten. For a thousand years, I hoped my female would find me since my searches were for naught.

And now I know why. She isn't immortal like my kind, and most likely hadn't been born more than a few *decades* ago. Still, as she pulled me toward her, our mate bond snapping into place the instant I first looked into her pretty blue eyes, the long, lonely years are nothing but a forgotten memory.

My life only truly began when I first saw my mate.

The males in my clan often talked of what it would be like when we found our females. She would recognize us the same way our hearts sang for her, and the physical bonding would be inevitable—and immediate. She would fall back, legs spread, inviting me into the warmth of her body, and I would finalize our mate bond as I filled her with my seed. We would never be separated after that, and I would no longer live alone.

It's all I've ever wanted, but my mate… no matter how I cajole her with words of her beauty, and promises of our future together, she gapes at me as if she expected another male than the one she received.

I tried to make her understand. "Mate," I told her. "My mate."

I even showed off my cock. She is the first female to see me unclothed, and though I would've conjured coverings of my own once I realized she whisked me from my bath, I want her to look at me. To see me. To know that everything I am is for her, and that I will endeavor to use my cock to give her pleasure.

My mating rituals are instinctive. I do what I can to make a claim and a vow all in one, but my odd little mate isn't only a wee mortal. She's frightened, and before she can release me from the bonds of her powerful magic, she runs.

She *leaves* me.

I can't follow. Her magic is too strong, and I have to accept that while the gods have blessed me with such an exquisite female, she is not demonkind. She is mortal, and everything I know about mating will have to change since she is Other.

I'm in her quarters. The room smells of freshness, of a cool breeze, of flowers that are doomed to never thrive in my corner of Sombra. While Mavro, Sombra's capital, is the only oasis in our arid world, as a mere artist and painter in a poorer clan, I live on the ashy outskirts of Nuit. Now that I have my mate, I'll need to find a town more fitting for my mortal flower.

Unless she invites me to stay with her here. I would. Already, I'm more inspired than I've been in centuries, and I've always wanted to visit other planes. In Sombra, the only way out is through a mate, and now I have her.

If only she'll have me…

Of all the Other mates, humans are considered forbidden fruit, all the sweeter because so very few of my kind are fated to mate with them. Mortal until we share our essence, they're so small. Breakable. If I forgot my strength for a single moment, I could hurt her. My pale-haired female would snap like a twig.

I will never forget my strength. And I will never make her experience anything but pleasure.

She will have to return. I hold onto that belief with a certainty that surprises me. For so many years, I've been complacent. I had nothing to look forward to.

Now I have forever within my grasp, and I'll do anything to keep it.

I know what I look like. I'm tall for even a Sombran, and I had hoped that would please my demoness mate. To discover that she's a human instead... of course I frightened her. I can't make myself any smaller—even in my shadow form I'm big —but I can promise that she is safe with me.

Time crawls by. The confines of the magic circle are barely big enough for me to turn around and take a few steps. Because I want to show my mate the respect she's owed, I stay standing so that I don't offend her when she finally returns to her quarters.

My ears prick up when I hear her approach what seems like an eternity later. Breathing deep, the soothing scent of flowers and a gentle breeze hits my soul. My mate is home.

My cock starts to stir again. I bat it with the back of my hand, willing it to behave. Though I noticed my mate being drawn to it, her scent had tinged with fear when she saw its size as I grew ready for her. Before I can attempt to explain that I am Malphas, that I am hers, and that we are made for each other, I need to keep her from fleeing me again. Staying limp and harmless is my only course of action.

Tell that to my randy cock. Instinct has me eager to pleasure my mate, to tie her to me for the rest of our endless life.

Human, I remember. Mortal. I must convince her to accept me.

"Fear not, little mortal," I rumble. "I will not harm you."

She doesn't understand the Sombran tongue. That much is already clear. Still, I must give her my word. An honorable male, I need to promise her *everything* in the hopes she'll give me the same.

Pity that it doesn't help. Even after I prove to her that I'm trapped inside of her ward until she releases me, she looks at me in fear and distrust. Lust, too, which makes my cock immediately harden. Though she's nervous, she's also aroused.

It's a start. Maybe she needed some time to accept that she's fated to a Sombra demon. It's probably as much a surprise to her as it was to me, though I have one advantage. I've spent my whole life hearing myths and legends about the mortals who cram an entire life into a mere century; even less, most of the time. Thanks to the duke's ministrations, she would've never known my kind exist. If she expected to mate a human, it must've been a revelation that I was the one who answered her summons.

She manifested me with her magic. She's my mate. And if I have to wait for her to be comfortable enough to accept me, I will.

I watch her closely. From the way she refuses to look away from me, I think she's grown used to my appearance; already I am smitten by hers. The fear has faded from her scent, though the delicious lust lingers.

She has no horns. Her skin is completely smooth with not a single defense to it. No claws. No fangs. She's everything that I'm not, and when she disappears to talk to another female out of my sight, I wonder what she's thinking now.

Will she leave me again?

She does not. In fact, when she returns to me, she seems different. More sure of herself. More determined.

It's as if she's made up her mind.

About me?

Gods, I hope so.

She starts acting even odder. Before long, I realize that she must be readying the both of us for our bonding.

Finally.

I must say, though, her mating rituals are so different than that of my people. Though I've heard about a demon taking a mortal for a mate, I've never known one personally who had. I know nothing of human courtship, either. If she wants to dust with me that strange-smelling powder and play music with a rounded wooden stick and a cooking vessel, then she must.

When that's done, she looks me up and down again. I wiggle my hips, my cock bobbing toward her, letting her know without words that I'm ready to mate when she is.

She immediately meets my gaze. When she speaks, her voice is a little more insistent than it was before, but I still don't understand.

Not yet, anyway.

She's as frustrated as I am at how difficult it is to communicate. With a huff that has her breasts rising and falling—and snaring my attention—she reaches behind her.

In the back pocket of her strange leg coverings, she keeps a small, rectangular box. Its top is made of glass, and it makes a gentle tapping sound when my mate pokes it with her fingertip.

She does that a lot.

She also spends a lot of time with this book of hers. Like now. Finally, my mate takes a seat. In her quarters, there are no chairs, but she climbs up on her bed. And while I'm eager to join her, I can't, but at least I can finally follow her lead and sit down myself.

Her mood lightens when I do. She must be impressed by my manners.

I smile, glad that I've finally made some progress with my mate.

She stares at my fangs before hurriedly dropping her gaze to the open book in her lap.

As my mate reads, I watch her. I can't help it. If I

didn't have to blink, I wouldn't. I want to always have her near, and if I can't touch her, I at least want to gaze upon her loveliness.

Though she's nothing like the mate I imagined, she's better because she's the one Fate set aside for me. The one I'm meant to love.

My forever.

I lose track of how long she's reading and I'm staring. Seconds, minutes, hours… so long as she's not running from me, I'm content to wait. Though, when she rises from her bed, holding the book open in her hands, I have to admit I'm curious to see what my odd little mate will do next.

Of course, I stand. It would be rude not to. And if my chest puffs up when her pretty blue eyes dip down to my straining erection, I can't help it. I want my mate to be pleased with my body.

After all, it's hers now.

She clears her throat before glancing down at her book. And then she begins to read out loud.

Her Sombran is atrocious, but my soul sings to hear her attempting to speak my tongue. She stumbles over the words, but I can still understand what she's saying.

My heart swells even more than my cock has.

A mate's promise. She's giving me the mate's promise. The unbreakable vow that will tie her to me for the rest of our lives—or until I release her from it, something that I will never, ever do.

She is my fated soulmate. The female I've spent an age waiting for, the one meant for me and me alone. From the moment I saw my odd little mate, she already had my vow. My eternal promise.

Now, I greedily accept hers.

"My soul will be yours."

Yes.

"My heart is in your hands."

And I'll treasure it always.

"Our lives will be forever intertwined…"

"Forever isn't long enough," I tell her. Lifting my hand, palm up, I offer it to my mortal. "To learn you, to know you, to love you, I'll need forever and one day more to be your male."

She glances up from her book, surprise written on her pale face. Those striking blue eyes—so lovely, yet so unusual—seem to widen. It's as though she hadn't expected me to interrupt her.

I shouldn't have. When your female is making her vow, a Sombra male stands quiet and strong. My mate… she already makes me weak. I don't mind. I'm proud to be hers, and even if she can't understand me, I want her to know.

I just need her to give me her essence. To move on to the next step of the mating ritual of my people. If she does, then I'll be able to explain myself.

There are only two things she has to do: finish her vow and touch me to share the essence of who she is with me.

Her magic keeps me contained. I'd burn if I fought against it, but it's only now that my mate has stopped looking at me in fear. Her terror is banked, and I don't want to be the male who brings it roaring back to life. She needs to trust me before she can truly mate me, and I can wait until she does.

Impatiently, yes, but it's already been more than a thousand years that I've longed for my one true mate. Knowing that she exists… knowing that I'm breathing the same air with her even if it's on a whole other plane… I'll do anything to prove to her that I'm worthy of her promise.

She must know. Deep down, she must already accept that we're fated to be together until the rest of time. I never thought my mate would be a human, but at least I knew the mortal race existed. Humans aren't allowed to know about Sombra unless they're the mate to one of my kind. As small and as delicate and as pale as she is, I must come as a shock to her. It was no wonder she was afraid, but she came back. She's talked at me in her human language, doing her strange mating ritual, and now she's making the mate's promise.

And, suddenly, I find it difficult to wait.

I don't push past the mystical ward surrounding me; I could, if I wanted to, but it wouldn't be worth breaking her spell, frightening her, and burning away my demonic form completely. Instead, I keep my hand inside the circle, imploring her to finish the vow.

After only a moment's hesitation, she moves until she's standing right before me. One hand is holding the book open in front of her, the other is slowly reaching out.

I go still. If I frighten my mate off now, I'll never forgive myself.

"Give it to me," I whisper softly. Yes. Finally. The mate bond is pulling her toward me, and I'm ready to receive her. "Touch me, my mate. I'll take everything—"

"I give you myself to you," she vows in Sombran, her voice gone throaty. "I give you *everything*."

I jolt. Whether it's from the electricity passing between her soft hand and my rough skin as she lays her palm over mine, or the pleasure I feel as her essence rushes through me, I'm not sure. This is the first time I've touched a female—*my* female—and I groan out the last few words in her language now that it's instinctively a part of me.

Just like everything my Shannon is.

"—you have."

CHAPTER 5
UP IN FLAMES

SHANNON

"**W**hat did you say?"

English. The monster spoke English.

I heard him. I know I did. But... but *how*?

I blame the spellbook. A couple of minutes ago, I got the grand idea to look at the true love spell again. I thought about reading the first part over before deciding against it. What if I did and the portal opened back up? Sure, I might be able to send this monster guy home again, but what if another one joined him? With my luck, I'd end up with two of them stuffed inside of the protective circle and an even bigger problem on my hands.

Figuring it was better not to risk it, I started to

read the bottom paragraph instead. There were only a few lines, and even if I wasn't sure what exactly it would do, I kept thinking about the star. Star means important, right? Like maybe this was the reversal spell or something?

It was worth a shot.

The weirdest thing happened, though. As I hurried through the spell, I felt my feet moving. Without even realizing what I was doing, I somehow reached for the monster this time.

And then he *freaking spoke English*.

Just like he does right now. "I was accepting your vow."

What's that supposed to mean? "In English," I repeat. "I didn't think you could speak English."

He runs his thumb over the top of my hand. That sucker is as thick as a sausage and almost as long as a hot dog. "I do now, thanks to you."

I barely pay attention to what he said in that deep, rumbling voice of his. I do notice that he has no accent—and isn't that really freaking weird?—before it dawns on me that he's still holding my hand.

I yank my whole arm back and away from him. What was I thinking? After spending the whole night trying to get rid of him, the big, red monster lifts his big old claw-tipped hand out to me again and I stupidly touch it as if to prove to myself that he's really real?

Why don't I step over the salt circle and offer

myself up to him on a silver platter? If I'm going to make it that easy for him to get to me, I might as well.

Okay. *Okay*. I lost my head for a second there, but I'm back. I have no idea why he suddenly understands English, but am I about to look a gift horse—well, shadow monster—in the mouth?

No. No, I am not.

We can talk. Great. I can find out who he is, what he's doing here, and how I can kick his giant ass out of my apartment. It would be better if he can tell me how to open another portal so that I don't give Mrs. Winslow a heart attack by making him leave through the front door, but… gonna be honest here… that's still on the table.

But, first, I gotta know—

What are you sounds kind of rude, so maybe I shouldn't start this conversation off with that. Instead, I say, "Who *are* you? What are you doing here?"

How can I get you to leave?

"My name is Malphas, and you are my mate."

I sputter. "I'm sorry, *what?*"

Still no accent, and if his smooth voice sends shivers down my spine, that has nothing to do with the possessive way he referred to me as his mate.

Nope. Not even a little.

"My mate," he repeats. "You summoned me to you, and now I'm here."

"I didn't summon you," I begin before my mouth clicks shut. Um. I might've summoned him. Not on purpose or anything—and there's no way he can be my "true love"—but there's no denying that I read the spell in that old book and he suddenly appeared.

I try another tactic. "Okay. You're here. How do I get you to go back? Because, sorry about the inconvenience and everything, but you got to go back."

His brow furrows. It's hard to tell with the bumps that erupt right over the bridge of his nose, but he looks confused.

That can't be good.

"You summoned me, my mate. Why would I go?"

Maybe because I'm not his mate?

"Malphas, look— hey, can I call you Mal?"

"Whatever you wish."

Whatever I wish? Right now, I wish he wasn't standing there buck-freaking-naked.

"Before this goes any further, can you, uh… can you cover up or something? I mean, I'm dressed. And you're not." Something occurs to me. Am I being insensitive by asking? For all I know, whatever Mal is, they don't even *wear* clothes. "Is that something you can do?"

"Does my mate request it? I'm yours. I don't mind if you want to see what I have to offer."

Oh, boy. I've already seen plenty. "That's okay. Just… if you don't normally wear clothes, do you want a blanket or something?"

"That won't be necessary." Mal waves his hand. A hazy black shadow trails behind his claw-tipped fingers, growing thicker and darker with every pass. I pointedly refuse to look any lower to see what he's doing until he drops his hand and, in a low voice, murmurs, "How is this?"

Sucking in a breath, I dare a peek. I don't know how he did it, but he wove himself a pair of tight black pants from the shadows he conjured. It doesn't really leave much to the imagination since they look like something a classic rockstar from the 70s might've worn, but at least his cock isn't threatening to poke out my eye.

"Better, yeah. Thanks."

"Don't thank me, my mate. I exist for your pleasure. All of it. Your wish, as ever, will be my command."

I can't help it. I guess you could say being a smart ass is my defense mechanism because I look the horned monster up and down, then say, "My wish, huh? What does that make you? A genie?"

"Genie?" he echoes. The glow in his brilliant gaze dims. "You're talking about the djinn."

Am I? "Okay."

"I am not djinn," Mal sniffs. Oh. Great. I guess I offended the seven-foot-tall monster in my room after all. "I am a demon from the Sombra plane."

Demon? Right. Like that's so much better.

I guess I was right when I thought he came from Hell.

At least I'm a little more prepared now that I

know what he is. I've watched a bunch of paranormal-themed shows. I've always been more of a werewolf girl, but I was a diehard Supernatural fangirl when I was still in high school. And the pentacle with the squiggles I drew kind of looks like a bootleg devil's trap when you add in the circle of salt I spilled around it.

Salt, too, was Sam and Dean's go-to when it came to battling demons, I remember.

"What about that?" I point to the circle of salt, then wiggle my fingers at the chalk drawing. "Are you really trapped inside of there?"

"It's the magic of the summoning. Your spell brought me to you and closed the portal between planes behind me. The salt is harmful to my kind. Unless you break the circle, this is where I'll stay."

So Supernatural got it right? Let's score one for scripted TV now! That makes it Shannon three, Mal zero.

I'll take it.

It's also good to know that he can only leave the circle if I let him out. As casual as this little chat is, I've never once forgotten for a moment that Mal is freaking seven feet tall, huge as hell, and he has both deadly-looking claws and intimidating fangs. I feel so much better knowing that he can't get to me unless I want him to.

Which I don't. Obviously.

Right?

I shake my head. Focus, Shannon. You got yourself into this mess, time to get yourself out.

"So what if I break the circle? Can you go back home then?"

When he says, "No", I have to admit I'm not even a little surprised, especially when he adds, "You brought me here. Only you can send me back."

If only I knew how to. The first time I tried to "do magic", Mal appeared. The second time, I found myself holding hands with a monster while he suddenly got the gift of gab.

Something tells me that, with my luck, the third time won't be the charm.

I still don't get it, though.

"But why you? How did I"—ah, jeez, this sounds so weird—"*summon* you? And I don't mean just you in general. I mean you in particular."

"I told you. You are my mate, as I am yours."

He keeps saying 'mate'. The more he does, the more I struggle with interpreting its meaning as 'friend' instead of something completely different.

Something I'm totally not prepared for.

Oh, yeah. I'm pretty good at ignoring things that are right in front of me. Like the erection I had Mal cover up, and the hungry look on his face earlier as he rasped out *uxor* in another language, not to mention the way he stroked my hand as if mesmerized…

"You must understand," rumbles the demon, drawing my attention back to him as if he can tell that

I'm seconds away from freaking out again. "The spell summoned me to you, but your promise… your vow… makes it so that I'll stay with you. Forever."

Yup. Total freak-out time. I should've known the pleasant conversation was some kind of a front, and that the absurdity of the moment was going to slap me in the face any second.

Forever…

It just did.

"Spell? What spell?" I do a half-crab walk, half-scoot around the perimeter of the salt circle, careful not to get within his reach again. The spellbook is on the floor. Snatching it, I wave it. "It's only a pretend spell in an old book. It wasn't supposed to *work*."

"Of course it did, my mate. You're full of magic."

"And you're full of shit!"

Mal scrunches his face, his horns dipping forward. His hair falls over his shoulder as he peers down at me in an expression so familiar, I could almost forget he's some kind of demonic creature.

Oh, great. I offended him again after all he did was try to answer the questions I asked him.

"Sorry." The word comes out as a mumble. As if this whole situation isn't weird enough, now I'm apologizing to a demon. "I just… I didn't think it would work."

"And your vow, mate? When you promised your-self to me?" His eyes start to glow again. "It's unbreakable."

The hell it is. "I didn't make any vow."

I think my denials have finally gotten the better of him. A scowl twists his features, erasing any hint of *human* I thought I found there before. "Why are you denying me?"

And… I'm out of here. Mal went from me hopefully thinking he was a figment of my imagination to a living, breathing demon who I might've just royally pissed off. I don't care if he can't leave the circle of salt. I need some freaking space.

I get as far as my open bedroom doorway when I hear a low groan that has me looking over my shoulder.

Only the memory of nosy Mrs. Winslow's earlier visit has me clamping my hands over my mouth to muffle my scream when I see the seven-foot-tall wall of fire where Mal was a second ago.

Just like the rush of hot air escaping the portal to Hell—or, I guess, Sombra—the heat from the flame slaps at me. Sweat immediately forms along my brow, and once I manage to get control of my scream, I start to cough.

Mal doesn't make a sound.

I don't know how long he burned. It felt like hours, though logically it was like two or three seconds before the fire suddenly extinguished, leaving the amorphous shadowy figure from earlier this afternoon in its wake.

"Be at ease, my mate," coos the monster in Mal's low voice. "The fire died."

The fire died, but Mal didn't.

"What are you," I blurt out, "immortal or something?"

Stupid question. He's a *demon*. He might be.

When he nods, as if I should've known that, I tuck that little nugget aside for later. So he's immortal, that doesn't change the fact that he went up in freaking smoke like that. "You were on fire!"

"Yes," he says soothingly, "and now I'm not."

"How?" It's all I can get out. No. Scratch that. "What the fuck just happened here?"

My floor is fine. No scorch marks as far as I can see, and now that he's in the same shadow monster form, complete with the runes running down his side, and his hazy shape, I can see there's no other damage.

Mal blinks. It's a slow blink, where he closes his eyes, hiding the golden glow from me for a second. When he opens his eyes again, they're not as bright, and he's back to being the muscular, red-skinned, *solid* demon.

All he says in answer is, "I am from Sombra."

"And? Is that supposed to answer my question? Or, I don't know, even mean anything to me?"

Actually, it does. Wasn't that the name of my book? *Grimoire du Sombra*... if a grimoire is a spellbook, the rest of it must mean "of Sombra".

Looks like I can't pretend that the spell was a dud

after all. It worked. I knew all along it did—only, I didn't manifest my true love. I manifested a demon straight out of Sombra, wherever that is.

"But you were on fire!" I remind him. I can't get over that part. "Does that happen often in Sombra?"

"Yes, but not like you think. What happened… it's our bond. I have your unbreakable vow and your essence. Until we finalize our mating, we can't be separated otherwise I'll burn. And when we do that, we *won't* be."

Unbreakable again; it's so much easier to dwell on that instead of how my breaking for my bedroom door caused him to light up like that. I'm about to remind him that he can't hold me to anything I said when I didn't understand his odd language when something a little more pressing occurs to me.

Not that I want to believe any of this, but considering my bedroom stinks of a mixture of burnt ash and rotten eggs, I don't see how I have any other choice. I mean, seeing things is one thing, but smelling them, too?

"Hang on… will I go up in flames, too? Like you did?"

"Are you Sombran? Do your people hail from Sombra?"

"Me? What? No. I'm from New Jersey."

"A mortal," he rumbles. "My delicious little human."

Delicious?

I stumble backward. Fear slams into me again and only the sight of seeing him burning like a damn fireball keeps me from bolting for the door. "You… you're not going to eat me, are you?"

"I'd give my left horn for a taste of you, my mate." His gaze drops to my crotch, leaving me in no doubt what his husky promise means. "I've waited an age to pleasure my female. You've summoned me to you. Must I really wait much longer? Will you continue to deny me?"

Oh. Instead of eating *me*, he wants to eat me out. Pleasure me.

My cheeks immediately heat up. I'm not on fire— not the way Malphas was—but the hungry look on his face has me feeling like I am.

He keeps saying 'mate'. At first, I was purposely being an idiot. Like, it could mean 'friend', right? But like how his view of eating me means something else to this hulking monster, being his mate isn't just his human buddy.

It's his human bride.

"Sorry, but that's gonna be a hard *no*."

His eyes light up again. "You can't have another male. I'd smell him on you."

And look at that. I'm sputtering again. But what do you expect? How else am I supposed to answer a statement like what he said to me a second ago?

Mal nods, his hair falling forward again. "You'll be mine. You promised."

Oh my god. I'm such a fucking idiot. How many times does he have to say 'promise' like that for a spark to go off inside of my brain?

Come on, Shannon. Where did you see that very same word written recently?

I'm still holding the stupid spellbook. Grateful I left The Beanery receipt as a placeholder, I quickly open up to the true love spell, then march over to Mal. Going up on my tip-toes, I shove it toward him.

"Can you read this?" I use my pointer finger to tap the words on the page, focusing on the second paragraph with *promise* written next to it.

"Yes. It's Sombran. You can't?"

I shake my head.

"I could give you my essence. If you accept it, you'll be able to understand my tongue the same way that I can understand yours now."

He wants to give me his essence? Yeah. I've heard that before. That's along the lines of my high school boyfriend begging me to let him put "just the tip" in, or my college boyfriend saying that he'll pull out right before he comes.

No, thanks.

I lift the book a little higher, moving it closer to him while still saying on my side of the salt. "Can you read it for me?"

"Of course, my mate."

"Shannon." The way he rumbles 'mate' like that is starting to make it a little harder now for me to forget what he's packing underneath his new shadow pants. And since he hasn't disappeared yet despite me really, really wishing he would, I probably should introduce myself at this point. "My name is Shannon."

"I know."

I don't even ask how. "Okay. Translate it please."

He does, my mouth opening in ill-disguised horror as I find out just what it was I said to him in his language before.

It never even occurs to me that he's making it up. He sounds so earnest as he repeats the vow I made in English, that I can't help but believe that he's telling the truth.

I promise that—
My soul will be yours.
My heart is in your hands.
Our lives will be forever intertwined.
I give myself to you.
I give you everything...

Oh, no. Oh, no, no, no.

I didn't do what I think I did—

Did I?

He can speak English now. I highly doubt he could before—and then I touched him and made this... this *promise* to him.

Oh, shit.

Somehow—and I'm still not sure how—I gave him my "essence", like he said I did. Without meaning to, I actually promised to be his mate. And if he believes it's unbreakable, and he's already batting a thousand when it comes to understanding what's going on way more than I do, then maybe my thoughtless promise really is.

You have *got* to be kidding me.

CHAPTER 6
PROGRESS

MALPHAS

That could have gone better.

As Shannon storms to the opposite side of the room—as far as she can go without triggering our bond, almost as if she instinctively knows the reach of it now—she throws her book on her bed.

A small yellow box was perched near the edge. When the book hits the mattress, the box bounces, falling to the floor. Two pieces of brightly colored chalk roll out.

I know chalk. In Sombra, we call it giz, and it's used by the demon mages in their spell work. Clan artists like me also use giz in our art, though my preferred medium is paint. Our giz—our chalk—only comes in white, black, greys, and reds, while our paints are imported from the brighter plane of Soleil and are colors not found in Sombra.

The human realm, I've decided, is much closer to Soleil than it is my shadowy home. It's cooler, for one, and the light outside far brighter than the darkness of Sombra. Plus the colors in my mate's quarters... I see shades I only dreamed of when attempting to create magic of my own out of my costly paints.

Until I met my Shannon, they were my pride and joy. Now? I only wish I had grabbed them before being summoned so that I could paint the beauty before me.

Even furious, she's the most striking vision I've ever seen.

I don't understand why she's so angry. She made her mate's promise, and I accepted it. I made mine, and when she takes my essence, then my seed, we'll be bonded.

And, yet, as she mumbles to herself, I have to admit that my human mate still doesn't seem too pleased at the promise of being mine.

She's angry, but I'm at a loss what to do. Mating is supposed to be easy. We recognize each other for who we are, and we cleave together.

Not my mate, it seems.

It happens. I've heard tales of stubborn mates— both males and females—who fought Fate. Who went against the gods' wishes and ignored the one creature made for them.

But even if a mate hesitates?

They won't for long.

Apart from the bond pulling us together and our vows making it impossible to be apart until we consummate our union, the mingling of our essences will make it so that my little mortal will crave my touch as much as I already ache for hers. So far, she's given me her essence; she offered it during her promise, cementing it when she touched my skin. If she willingly accepts mine in return, we're as good as fully bonded.

But that, I fear, will not be happening tonight.

Shannon runs her fingers through her fair hair, swooping its weight over her shoulder. Spinning on her heel, she points at me again. "Look. What's done is done, right? At least until tomorrow."

Tomorrow? "What's tomorrow?"

She shakes her head. "Another day. I'll deal with this… with *you*… then. Right now? I'm tired. I'm hungry and I'm tired, and I probably shouldn't have had that second coffee, because I'm really feeling the crash now."

I know her language, but that doesn't mean I understand everything she says. Coffee… to me, I think of javits, a brewed drink that is also a stimulant. Drink enough javits and I've been known to get stuck in my shadow form because I'm buzzing too much to return to my demon shape. And crash? Ah… that must be how, when the javits burns out of us, we return to our quarters and sleep until the next moon.

I nod. "Then you should fill your belly, then go to bed. Rest and know that I will keep you safe."

Her gaze narrows. "What about you? Do you go to bed? Demons… do you, like, lay down and sleep?"

What kind of question is that? As much as I wish it was otherwise, I doubt it's an invitation to join her. Maybe she's eager to learn more about me?

I will tell her everything I can.

"Yes. It's nearly always dark in the shadows of Sombra, especially in Nuit, but my clan retires when the shadows are at their darkest."

"So you're tired, too? You'll go to sleep now?"

No, but she doesn't need to know this. "If that's what you want me to do."

"On the floor? Because, sorry, but I only have the one bed, and I don't think you'll fit on my couch."

She's still nervous. When she mentions her bed, her scent flares with her unease. Despite her promise, she doesn't see me as her mate the same way that I do her.

That just means I have to work harder to prove that no male will be better for her than I. And if I have to stay within the confines of her protective circle to do so, I will. Gladly.

As a clan artist, I'm not as wealthy as Duke Haures, his soldiers, or even Apollyon, the leader of my clan. Still, I have enough to buy my paints, and to have a home with a bathtub, a bed of my own, and access to the Sombra fire pits to sear my meat for supper. It's been centuries since I had to lie on the floor instead of on my feather-stuffed mattress, but to be this close to my mate, I wouldn't think twice.

"I will."

"Because you have to be near me, right?"

She says it as a question, but we both know it's more a statement. Unless she wants me to burn in her home, we need to stay close.

"Yes."

Her fingers pluck at a stray strand of her hair. She's nervous again, but still bold enough to meet my gaze as she says, "Can I trust you?"

One day, when she knows every inch of me, she'll understand how ridiculous that question is. There will be no male more loyal, more true, and more of a protector for her than I.

I could tell her, but she won't believe me. If I tell her that it's impossible for me to lie to my mate, she'll only assume that that is also an untruth.

So, instead, I answer her question with one of my own.

"Do you believe you're my mate?"

"I…"

She hesitates, biting the corner of her mouth as she thinks it over. It takes everything I have not to groan at how effortlessly sexy she is to me. I feel as if we're on the edge of something momentous, and if I remind her how desperate I am for her touch, I'll scare her away again. I'm sure I will.

After a few seconds where I struggle to ignore the renewed ache in my heavy sack, she says tentatively, "I think that *you* believe that I am."

That's the best I'm going to get right now. I will take it.

"I do. You are my mate. Sombra demons… we only get one. Whether you believe that or not does not change the truth. Can you trust me? You can trust me to watch over you, to protect you, and to eventually love you with everything that I am. To harm you would be to harm myself."

Every word I said is true. From the moment her spell found me, bringing me to her side, my life is no longer my own. I live for my mate.

Shannon lifts her hand to her mouth, fingers pressing lightly against her lips. She doesn't say anything, and I wonder if I went too far. In Sombra, a demoness would take a confession like that as her due. Then again, a demoness would not doubt that Fate chose me for her.

It will be tricky to convince my human mate that we're fated. She doesn't *sense* our tie the way that I do. And like humans are mortal, they don't sense the mate bond the way demonkind can. It's what makes them so unique—and such a rare prize for a male like me.

I understand. All the legends and the fables of

males who sacrificed everything for their human mate… I know what it is to have the promise of my forever dangling out of the reach of my claw. I'd rise up against Duke Haures, I'd risk chains and torment, I'd break all of our ancient laws if only for a single taste of my mate—and I'd do it with a smile on my face.

She will be my greatest challenge. If I fail, I have nothing. But if I succeed? My prize will be *priceless*.

"I know you don't feel what I feel," I say, my voice a rumble deep in my chest, "but I hope you will see that I would've found my way to you regardless. I've waited my whole life for you. It was only a matter of time, my mate. So even if you can't trust me now, know this. I will not rest until I've earned that trust. I vow it."

A soft snort escapes my delicate mate. I already adore the sound and can't wait for her to make it again. "Another vow?"

I nod. "As many as it takes, Shannon."

Suspicious and wary as she is, my mate is also a soft touch with a kind heart. I know that. I know everything about her, but it would be wrong to use her secrets against her. So when she sighs and says, "I might be a moron for falling for all that, but I can't leave you like this," before reaching down to swipe at the salt with her hands, I stop her.

She has all of the magic. As she proved when she touched me earlier, she can cross the circle with ease.

Me? I can not. The sigils are designed to react to the power in my people that allows us to go from demon form to shadow and back. I could use force against her magic, but I'll have to pay the price.

For my mate, to prove just how trustworthy a male I am, I'll pay it.

I push through the border, gently encircling her pale wrist with my long fingers.

She sucks in a breath. My mate isn't frightened, though she is surprised. "What are you doing?" she demands. "I thought you can't get out of the circle."

I'm not supposed to, but this was important.

"Please." Already I can feel the fire. I must make this quick. "If it makes you feel better, leave it. When I earn your trust, I'll earn my freedom. 'Til then, I'll stay inside your spell."

Shannon laughs. It's not a pleasant laugh. It's actually quite hollow. I frown, fighting the urge to drop her hand only because she hasn't tried to pull herself out of my grasp.

"Go figure," she mutters. "Of all the demons I summoned to my bedroom, I get the one who thinks he's a gentleman. I thought you just vowed that I could trust you."

"I'm not a man, my mate," I remind her gently. "I am a Sombra male. And you can trust me, but that doesn't mean I'll roam free if you don't wish it."

"Whatever. And stop calling me your mate."

Why would I? "But you are."

"Forget it. I was trying to be nice. But if you want to stay in there, fine. I won't stop you."

She jerks her hand back. I immediately release her, but it's too late. Whether her anger ignited her magic or I pushed it too hard, my own hand pays the price for my greed. I knew better than to break the circle, and I did so anyway if only to touch her a few moments longer.

My hand catches fire. From the tips of my claw to my wrist, the part of my body on the other side of her circle is completely in flames. Pulling my hand inside of the protective circle, I shake it. The damage is already done. My demon hand has burned away to shadow.

It's not like the warning from before. That was our unfinished bond engulfing me when she went too far. This? This is what I get for refusing to respect the old magics. I will need to heal before I can use my hand again, and without the clan healer, that could take some time.

Even worse, I upset my mate.

When the fire started, she yelped, backing away from me. She's only gone for a few seconds, though, before Shannon comes marching back, her hands on her hips.

"What the hell? You said you only go up in flames when I leave you. I'm right here!" Her sky-blue eyes flash angrily, like lightning across her face. "Are you doing this on purpose? I won't feel bad, you know. If you're doing it to yourself, you deserve to be on fire."

She isn't wrong.

"I guess you could say that I did," I admit. "I knew what would happen if I tested your spell, but I did anyway. Without you releasing me from the circle, I was bound to burn eventually. And not just my form, but my essence."

And *that* does hurt me.

Her expression softens as if she knows what I'm not saying. "Ah, crap. You mean... you burned because of me?"

I never want her to shoulder blame that is mine. "I chose to reach out of the circle. Not you."

"Yeah, but only because I've kept you trapped in there for hours now. You're probably hungry. And"— she absently waves toward my cock—"if you got one of those, you probably have to pee, too. You only tried to stop me because you didn't want me to be scared. Well, I'm not scared anymore, but I am a big jerk. Come on." She strides purposely toward the circle, using the toe of her foot covering to make a break in the salt. "Just don't eat me or anything, okay?"

Immediately, the magic that kept me within her circle fades. I'm free to move, but I stay where I am so as not to spook Shannon. She says she's not scared, and I can scent that she's telling the truth. Nervous, perhaps, though my mate likes to tease.

Why else would she think I would *eat* her? Or any human, for that matter?

"Of course not," I say solemnly. "Humans are meat. I would never eat one."

She blinks. "So, what? You're a vegetarian?"

In her language, vegetarian means plant-eater.

"No." I smile, making sure she can see my fangs. My mother used to tell me that they were my best feature, and since Shannon purposely avoids my cock, I will try to impress her another way. "See? I can tease, too."

Shannon stares at me. "That's effed-up, Mal."

Mal. No one's ever shortened my name before. In Sombra, it would be seen as an insult to use any other name but the one I was given. Still, from all I've learned about my mate so far, I can tell she has no ill intent.

"I will eat all the plants the human realm has to offer if it pleases you, my mate."

"Shannon," she corrects.

"Of course." To continue to please my mate, I must remember to use her name. But… if I'm 'Mal', should I give her a name of her own? "Would you like me to shorten your name, too?" I ask. "You could be my 'Shan'? Or, perhaps, 'Non'?"

My mate wrinkles her nose. "Um, no. Shannon is fine."

"Very well." I nod. "I would still prefer you to call me 'Mal'."

Actually, I'd prefer she call me her *uxor* in my tongue, or her *mate* in hers, but until then, I choose the shortened version of my name. I am not in Sombra—at least, not until the next gold moon—and I want Shannon to claim me any way she can. As my one true mate, it's only fitting that she uses a name for me that no other soul has before.

She gives me a curious look, then shrugs. "Whatever floats your boat."

In her own way, my mate has said, "As you wish."

I grin to myself.

Progress.

CHAPTER 7
A DEMON'S KISS

SHANNON

Rolling over in my bed the next morning, I've barely stretched myself the rest of the way awake when I hear a deep, male voice murmur, "Good morning, my mate."

There goes the last of my grogginess. My eyes spring wide open, my hand snatching my blanket to cover me all the way up to my chin. I went to bed in a t-shirt and a pair of sweats that I only changed into after I made the monster turn around, but there's something about the timbre of his voice that has me shivering like I'm freaking naked.

I scoot back, slamming into my headboard as I search for him. Seven feet tall and as muscular as a linebacker, I shouldn't be able to miss him—and I don't. He's awake, too. Folding up his huge body, he's sitting on my floor, watching me. The pillow I gave him, plus the blanket, is piled next to him.

When I catch his eye, they begin to glow. His lips curve, revealing his fangs. As I gape at him, he lifts one monstrous hand, waving at me.

I don't know what to do. I might as well wave back.

So… I guess I have to face the obvious. The chalk, the spellbook, the demon… it wasn't a dream like I hoped. It really happened. Mal is really here. He's still in his demon form, and unless I'm used to it, my room doesn't stink like rotten eggs anymore so he must've spent the entire night nearby.

Damn it. This would be so much easier if he really was something I made up.

Hey. Can you blame a girl for hoping? Since he's not, I have to actually figure out what to do now.

Great. Just freaking ducky.

"Did you sleep well?" rumbles Mal.

Strangely enough, I *did*.

It took everything I had to finally fall asleep last night—and, okay, maybe a sleeping pill or two—since, no matter how tired I was, going unconscious with a *monster* in my bedroom was quite possibly the dumbest thing I could do. I realize that now. Last night was different, though. I'd justified it by telling myself that either Mal proved that I really could trust him, or he proved he couldn't. Either I would have a peaceful night's sleep, or I would wake up to him gobbling me up. The not knowing was worse than choosing to have him stay close by.

So far, he passed the test. Beneath my blanket, I wiggle my toes, making sure that I didn't wake up missing any pieces; my hands look okay, and apart from the lingering grogginess from the sleeping pill, I feel fine.

"Yeah," I answer, dropping my blanket. I run my fingers through my bedhead, trying to tame my unruly hair. "I did. You?"

"I've never spent a better eve. Thank you."

He's thanking me for letting him sleep at my feet like some kind of pet. Poor guy. Not only does Mal talk kind of weird—sometimes he sounds old-fashioned, while other times he sounds almost human—but I don't know how bad his hellish world must be if that's the best night he ever had.

When I point that out to him, Mal shrugs. "That has nothing to do with Sombra."

I raise an eyebrow. "Oh? Then what *does* it have to do with?"

"You, my mate. This was my first night in your quarters. I got to protect you while you slept. That's a mate's honor, and you granted it to me. That's why I had to thank you."

I guess I should've known better than to start this

conversation. He's still on this "you're my mate" BS from last night, and nothing I do or say is going to change his mind. He's convinced that we're supposed to fuck—he says 'mate', but we both know he means 'fuck'—and apart from the fact that he's a *demon* from another world, with that club between his legs, there's no way it'll work. It's like shoving a cucumber inside of a wedding band. It won't fit.

What's even weirder is that he seems to think we're compatible. Who knows? Maybe we are. He definitely has a cock, even if it looks like someone pumped it full of air before stretching it out like a freaking balloon animal. Shoot, it even looks like a snake. But just because he has the equipment to get down, it doesn't mean that I should go for a ride.

Now, I'm not a prude. I've always been the type of chick who's willing to try anything once in the bedroom; if I like it, I'll do it again and again. I like pleasure, and even though I hadn't had a lover in a few years, that doesn't mean I've given up on feeling good. I have my romance novels with my book boyfriends, and a drawer full of toys that keep me satisfied.

But even if I decide to give Mal a try before I send him home, I'm afraid I'll rip myself in half trying to handle his monster-sized dick. And that's nothing compared to the idea that, if I give in to my horny side and sleep with a demon, what happens next?

Something tells me that he won't take a pity screw, then wave goodbye.

Do demons have STDs? Could I get knocked up with a half-human, half-demon baby?

Would my future child have *horns*?

See? This is why I had to take a sleeping pill last night. Once I was lying down, I started to wonder what it would be like to invite Mal into my bed. Sad, I know, but the way he looked at me as if I'm his fondest dream come true was a boost to my esteem I hadn't known I needed. I actually thought about it… but then reality came crashing in—and I don't just mean how I thought about any future kids with Mal.

Monster-fucking is something I've read about in some of the high-steam books I either buy on my e-reader or when Kennedy gets a donation of racy romance. It's not *real*. Take alien romance, for example. If freaking ET decided to blast me into space, I shouldn't want to sleep with him. And if a demon tries to sell me this idea that I'm his one true mate, I should be running for the door, not trying to figure out the mechanics of how I could make it work.

Oh. Right. I tried running, and what happened? Mal went up in flames.

I'm still not sure if he did it on purpose or not. My gut says no, but that's probably because I want to believe that letting him sleep in my room wasn't as crazy an idea as it was. Either way, there's no denying that he was on fire, and if I can keep him from burning again, I will.

"I only let you stay because, if I kicked you out of my room, you'd go up in flames," I remind him. "That's all."

"Ah. So you do care about me," he says, his massive chest puffing out in pride. While he still has on those tight shadow pants as he did last night, Mal never conjured a shirt, leaving me helpless but to trace his sculpted muscles with my gaze.

I should've remembered. Shannon is horny in the morning.

Whoops.

Another rumble deep inside of him before he asks me, "Do you like what you see? Come. Touch your male. Learn him. You don't have to be afraid of me."

"I'm not," I shoot back, snorting as I shove my blanket away from me. I'm not lying, either. I stopped being afraid of him sometime last night. "And I don't care about you. I don't even *know* you. But even if you were my worst enemy, I couldn't let you burn like that. It's not right."

He beams over at me. "You are a kind soul, my mate."

I huff. "My name is Shannon."

"Yes. But you are also my mate."

I'm not going to argue. Let him think what he wants since those horns of his are definitely attached to a thick skull. If I couldn't convince him last night, it would only be a waste of breath this morning after I let him out of his trap and allowed him to sleep in my room.

His horns still on my mind, I glance over at them as I slowly pull myself out of bed. The second I'm standing, Mal gracefully maneuvers himself to his bare feet, standing tall. Of course, now that means my line of sight is locked right on his junk.

Even with the shadow pants he's wearing, my pervy mind can make out the outline of his dick. I gaze at it for longer than I should, then quickly tear my gaze away. Looking upward would be safer, I think, and I settle on his face.

I don't want Mal to think that I'm afraid of him. If I keep looking away because I find myself drawn to checking him out, he might take it the wrong way. So I look at his face, and when his eyes lock on mine, I hold the stare for a few seconds as I stumble toward my dresser.

This morning, I'm a little more used to his appearance. The pointed ears. The slight bumps along his brow. The deep red skin. The gleaming yellow eyes. He's still completely alien, but his humanoid features and the way he can speak English now makes it easy to think of him as a person instead of as a monster.

Am I attracted to him? That's a loaded question. He has parts that I can't help but appreciate—and not only his massive demon cock. He's huge, but he's proportional, and even if some women aren't into the whole Arnold Schwarzenegger, muscle-bound hero from old 80s movies, I dig it. I dig lean, pretty boy, poetic types like Derek of The Beanery, too, but something about a guy who looks like he can lift me up over his head and bench me revs my engine a bit.

That's not all.

I look at his mouth. Set aside the inch-long fangs that sometimes overhang his bottom lip. He has a pretty mouth. His lips are lush, and when he smiles, it gives life to his whole face.

I don't know how long I'm staring at his mouth, marveling over it. I'd gotten up to grab a change of clothes from my dresser, but before I know it, Mal has moved.

And the demon is *fast*.

He moves right in front of me. Stunned by how quickly he was able to go from the foot of my bed to the side, I have no choice but to back against the dresser to avoid him.

I did exactly what he wanted me to.

Suddenly, his arms are a cage around my body. His hands stretch around me, gripping the dresser, his chin bowing into his chest so that Mal completely surrounds me. With his height and his bulk, I'm trapped—but I'm not afraid.

I probably should be. I mean, his muscles are as big as my head! If he wanted to, he could probably snap me in half, and even if I was keen on letting him burn, his speed is inhuman.

If he chased me, I'd never escape him.

I gulp, a little horrified by how the idea of Mal chasing me just turned me way on.

What the hell, Shannon? That's not hot. Definitely not hot.

Maybe it's a little hot.

"What…" My voice is shakier than I want it to be. I swallow, then try again. "What are you doing?"

"Getting my mate ready for me."

What?

"I'm not your mate."

I sound like a broken record, but it's all I can get out. No *get away from me*. No *leave me alone*. As if I belong in his arms, I don't even try to fight him— though, deep down, I know that, if I did, he'd back up immediately.

Mal grins. "Ah, little mortal. *Shannon*. You are."

The demon has no right sounding as seductive as he does. Even more intoxicating is the way that he slowly moves his hands down from the dresser, reaching for me.

My heart rate kicks up.

Okay. Who the heck is this lothario demon, and what did he do to Mal?

I don't even realize that he's given me the chance to duck away from him until he finishes his slow movements by gripping my waist. His fingers are a scorching brand even through my nightshirt as he slowly tugs me closer to him.

"Wait a minute, big guy." I slap his hands, quick enough that I don't get burned by his heat, but he keeps them planted against my hips. And, still, I don't try to get away from him as I ask wildly, "Ready? Ready for what?"

He bends his knees slightly. "For this."

CHAPTER 8
SUNFLOWER

SHANNON

Before I know it, the demon has bridged any gap between us. Tugging me against him, pulling me up so that I'm standing on my tippy-toes, Mal angles his head, closing his bright eyes right in time to come in for a kiss.

I'm too shocked to react at first. Then, when I do, I start to kiss him back—but not for long. Maybe a second or two before I realize what the heck is going on.

I rip my mouth away from his. "What are you doing?" I snap up at him. "You can't just kiss someone like that!"

Mal frowns. "You can't? But you wanted me to."

"What? No, I didn't!"

Yes, I did.

Still stunned, I finally realize that he's holding me. That's gotta stop. I shove him in his big, muscular chest. The heat coming off of him makes me wince when I hit him, and he's so hard, it's like pounding a brick wall.

Like I thought before, the second I *try* to get away from him, he immediately backs off. There is no hesitation. Mal bows his head, his lips pulled down while the gleam in his eyes tells me that he doesn't regret kissing me even a little.

Okay. So it was a nice kiss. I wasn't expecting it, so it wasn't all right that he did that, but it wasn't bad.

Not that I'm going to admit that to Mal.

But do I have to?

He knew I wanted to know what it was like to kiss him. *How?*

"Can you read my mind?" I demand. "Can demons do that?"

"No. At least, not demons from Sombra. But even if I could, I wouldn't have to. I *know* you."

"Oh, come off it," I scoff. "We barely met. You don't know anything about me."

I shouldn't have dared him. Tracking me around the room, taking two steps for each one I take away from him, Mal proves that maybe he does.

"You're Shannon Crewes. Twenty-nine human years old."

I stop when my back hits the wall right next to my

headboard. I literally can't go any farther unless I want to scamper across my bed.

Instead, I jerk my chin up at him. "So? All you had to do was go snooping in my purse and read that on my driver's license."

Well, first the demon had to know where my purse was, and that I kept my license in my wallet. Plus, I don't know if time runs the same in Sombra as it does in the human world, so would he see my DOB and know how to figure out my age?

But those are all logical thoughts that I quickly shove out of my head. He knows my name and age because he got that info from my license, that's all.

"You're good. Kind. A soft heart, and I'm probably not worthy of being your male. But I am."

"You think so."

"I know so."

I'm getting tired of this. "Right. Just like you know me."

"You need me to tell you more? Of course. Your favorite color is orange, a shade you can find mingled with the red dust of Sombra. You are a meat-eater like I am, but, also like me, you're not a hunter. You get your meals from"—his brow furrows—"something called Stop and Shop. You love to cook, but you hate to clean. I will do so for you, my mate. You work with clients to earn coin, and you collect books. Water falling from the sky makes you smile. I know that I'm not the first male you've mated, but I will certainly be the last.

"And," he adds, showing off a pair of fangs that shouldn't be anywhere near as sexy as they are, "you were wondering what it would be like to kiss me."

My mouth falls open. Why couldn't he be wrong? Why couldn't he say that I'm an illiterate chick who is both a docile virgin that gets her rocks off scrubbing dishes? Maybe that Shannon is a fan of pink, and she gets annoyed when it rains because it'll ruin her hair-do.

But no. Mal was able to pin every detail about me, down to the fact that I buy my groceries at Stop and Shop instead of Whole Foods because it's cheaper.

I close my mouth, my teeth making an audible *click* when they hit. For a second, I don't know what to say, until I finally mutter, "I should put you back in the salt circle for good."

"You could. I'd go gladly if you really wanted me to. So long as you keep it in your quarters." His lips curve. Damn it, now that I know what they feel like pressed against mine, they're even more lush. "I liked watching you sleep."

Hang on—

That was creepy, right?

I remember the folded blanket with the pillow placed on top. Now that I think about it, he was already wide awake when I got up, but did he really go ahead and fold the blanket?

Or did he not go to sleep at all?

"Did you stay up all night?"

"Sombra demons only need three or four hours of rest at a time," he says, completely disregarding my question. "Besides, I was occupied."

"Occupied?" I echo, snorting again. "What? Being a creeper and watching me sleep?"

"Yes," he says without a hint of shame. "But also because of this."

Mal gestures at the floor closer to the far side of my bed. From my angle, I have no idea what I'm looking at, and I wonder if this is another way to knock me off my guard. To see what he's pointing at, I'd have to walk by him.

They say curiosity killed the cat. Let's hope it doesn't do anything to Shannon because, damn it, I kind of want to see why he stayed up last night.

"I have to go to the bathroom anyway," I mumble, inching my way by him.

Smart demon. He switches to his shadow form right as I go past him so that he doesn't accidentally brush against me with his bulk. His innate warmth still rushes off of him, and I feel a heat-filled breeze caress the side of my neck and my face as I scoot past him, but he doesn't grab me again.

Once I've gone around the edge of the mattress, I glance down.

And I stare.

When I bought the pack of chalk yesterday, it

came with five colors: pink, yellow, blue, green, and white. Glancing down at the second drawing on my floor, you would think there were more. A skilled artist had managed to take the five colors and create a stunning portrait of…

"Is that me?"

It's close enough. The yellow hair, the blue eyes, the pink cheeks… I guess this is me. Only, this is what I would look like after a round or two with Photoshop.

The portrait is absolutely gorgeous.

From somewhere to my side, I hear Mal say, "I could've slept, my Shannon, but I finally found my mate after waiting so long. Forgive me if I wanted to bask in your beauty for a little longer."

A less confident woman would doubt he meant what he said. Even if that was me, all it took was one look at the portrait to know that he saw me as even more beautiful than I ever did.

He drew this. While I slept and hoped I'd wake up to discover this was all a bad dream, he found the colored chalk I bought and etched an image of my face on my floor.

"I—" I'm dazed. If the kiss knocked a few screws loose, this has broken me. I shake my head. "I'm going to take a shower."

I have an attached bathroom. We already tested how far I can go before Mal says our "bond" is stretched to its limits. So long as he moves to the other side of my room, I can have some privacy in the bathroom without him bursting into flames.

Without looking at Mal, I make a break for it. If he starts to spark because he doesn't move in time, that's his problem.

I already have plenty.

OH, BOY. I MADE A BOO BOO.

What was I thinking? It's a safe bet to say that I wasn't. I was so quick to hide in my bathroom, hoping the monster respected my privacy enough not to follow me, that I forgot to finish grabbing my clothes.

It's partly Mal's fault. His kiss caught me off guard. I'm still pissed that he just took the initiative to grab me like that, but I'd be lying if I said he was wrong. I *was* wondering what it would be like to kiss him. That didn't mean I gave him permission, and after the way I gave him hell for it, I don't think he'll try anything like that again.

Waking up to him watching me messed me up. The heat flooding through me at his gentle kiss made it worse.

And then I saw the portrait.

I needed some space. I needed to get away from Mal for a moment, and if staying beneath the spray of water until it ran icy cold was what I had to do, I did it. I even yanked the handle to the right to cool off when I first jumped into the shower.

Mal runs hot. Each time I've touched him so far, I've noticed that. I guess it has something to do with being a Sombra demon—or maybe a demon in general, for all I know—but he's noticeably hotter than I am. I'm not on fire, but after our close encounter, I'm definitely burning up.

And now I'm in trouble.

I live alone. I have since I was twenty-three and I moved to Jericho for my job. The promotion I got was enough of a pay bump that I could finally afford to live on my own without any roommates. Still, old habits die hard, and I tend to gather all of my clothes together with me and bring them into the bathroom to get ready after a shower.

Did I do that today? No. No, I did not.

Mal distracted me. I'd been heading for my dresser when he made his move, and after I warned him not to do that again, he showed me the chalk portrait on the floor. I never grabbed my clothes which means that, as I shake off the chill from my shower, I have nothing to cover up with except for my towel.

I normally keep a stack of towels in my bathroom. I have just enough to last me between loads of laundry, but when I go too long, I eventually get stuck with the smallest towel I have. Actually, calling it a towel is being generous. It's a glorified washcloth that just about covers me from boob to butt—and that's if I hold it tight.

Wouldn't you know? I was supposed to go to the laundry room last night, but I played around with that old spellbook instead. That means I'm down to the teensy, eensy towel and no choice but to use it.

Well. No. I *could* call out to the demon and see if he could pass me something to wear. But since that means I would be allowing him to go through my drawers, giving him free rein to handle my freaking panties with his claws, I refuse to do that.

Baby towel it is.

Sucking in a deep breath, wrapping the towel snugly around my boobs, I think about spending the rest of my life naked in the bathroom, then reach for the doorknob with my free hand. Maybe if I wasn't hungry for breakfast, I might've, but when it's between possibly embarrassing myself and going hungry, my belly wins.

The second I step into my room, I point at Mal while using my other hand to keep the towel closed tight.

"Don't get any ideas," I warn. "I just need to get some clothes."

Mal's standing about five feet away from me. The second he sees me, his eyes begin to glow like a freaking flashlight as he stares at me. He doesn't make a move toward me, though, and if he's drooling, it's whatever. I show off more skin when I wear a bikini down the Jersey shore, so it's not like he can really see much that I'd normally hide.

Still, he *is* staring.

I snort. "Eyes up here, Mal."

He lifts his hand, wiping at his mouth. For a second, I really think that he *is* drooling, before he gestures with a shaky claw to my side.

"What is that? On your arm?"

I glance down at my tattoo. Is that what he was staring at? Not my boobs?

Oh. Okay.

Until now, my arms have been completely covered up. My legs, too. He wouldn't have seen the fleur de lis I have tattooed on the inside of my ankle, or any of my flowers. Makes sense that he would be drawn to the sunflower on my arm first. It's the biggest piece I have.

"This? It's one of my tattoos. My ink." Shouldn't he know that already? And why does he look so surprised? "What? Don't you have body art in Hell?"

"It's Sombra," Mal corrects without a hint of irony. Huh. I guess he can't tell that I was teasing. "And we do. Males mark themselves with silver ink across their chest after they've taken a mate." With the tip of his claw, he gestures to his brawny chest. "I will etch 'Shannon' into the space right here. That way it matches how your name is branded on my heart."

Oh my god. Right when I thought we might have a normal conversation—with him obviously being some kind of artist, and me an art aficionado—he starts up again.

I roll my eyes. "You do that."

"I didn't know that humans marked themselves," Mal says, dropping the 'mate' crap if only for a moment. Huh. Maybe he really can tell my mood. "It's not a mate mark, though."

Maybe not.

"Nope. It's just something I liked so I had it put on my body. We do that here. It's a little something we call free will. No Fate involved," I add. "You should look into it before I find a way to send you back home."

Again, Mal proves that he's a smart demon. He completely disregards my last comment as he says, "It's a flower. A yellow one."

"Right." I tap the design that curves around my left bicep. "It's a sunflower."

My mom's a huge fan of them. When I got my first tattoo at eighteen, it was a delicate daisy chain that wrapped my right ankle. Daisies are my favorite flowers, and then I got a small rose on my back in memory of my paternal grandmother, Rosie. By then, I kind of had a flower theme going, and I got this one in honor of my mom.

"Blooms in the sun," Mal says, his tone turning reverential tone. "Full of magic."

Um. Sure.

Whatever.

SHANNON

"If you're done ogling my ink, I'd like to get dressed."

He bows his head. I can still sense him watching me, but he moves aside again to let me make my way to my dresser.

This time I gather my clothes together without any incident.

I guess you could say my style is pretty boring. During the week, our office dress code is business casual. On the weekends, I stick to t-shirts in the spring, tank tops in the summer, and the same hoodie with a skull design for both winter and fall. Since it's the tail end of spring, I grab a grey tee, a pair of jeans, some underwear, then sidle past Mal to head back to the bathroom.

"Let me finish up in here," I tell him, "then you can do whatever it is you have to do."

He nods, and just as he's opening his mouth to say something, I slam the door in his face.

Oops.

I take my time. The bathroom has become my personal sanctuary since I inadvertently opened my apartment up to my new demon roomie, and while I hope to get rid of him as soon as I can, for now this is as far as I can get away from him. I pull on my clothes, blow dry my hair, even put on a little make-up. When I start to wonder if I have time to give myself a pedicure, even I think I might've taken this too far.

Going back to the room, I'm not even a little surprised to see that Mal is still standing there, waiting for me.

I hold the door open for him. "Your turn."

"Thank you, my Shannon."

I open my mouth, think better of it for a heart-beat, then shrug. "No problem, Mal."

I'LL GIVE CREDIT WHERE CREDIT'S DUE. UNLIKE ME, Mal doesn't drag out his time in the bathroom. I taught him how to use the toilet last night—and discovered that, in Sombra, they have something pretty similar. Same with the sink and the shower, though he made a point to tell me that he prefers tubs large enough for two.

Because of course he does. Can the demon get any more heavy-handed with his hints?

Actually, no. Strike that. I shouldn't give him any ideas.

After about five minutes, he comes out with his hair wet, his face rubbed clean, and his hands dripping stray droplets on my floor. I have to bite my tongue to keep from snapping at him to stop the water away from the chalk drawing. I didn't even have to. Mal's obviously a seasoned artist and he gives the portrait a wide enough berth with both his shadow-covered feet and his wet hands that it stays pristine.

Together, we go into the kitchen. I let him see it briefly the night before when I made a pair of ham and cheese sandwiches for us—while working hard not to think about how crazy it was I was feeding cold cuts to a demon—and, this morning, I fry up some bacon. I keep remembering how he said he was a meat-eater like me, and how he liked the ham from dinner. Can't go wrong with a little bacon, right?

Once we're finished, and Mal insists on washing our plates for me, I have to break the news to him. "Okay. Breakfast is done. You know where the bathroom is. I can show you how to work the TV so you're not bored, but I have to go out for a few minutes. I'll be back as soon as I can."

"I don't know what a TV is," says Mal, "but I won't need it. I'm coming with you."

"Um. No. You gotta stay here."

He shakes his head. "Where you go, I go. You're my mate."

Screw that. "Well, in case you forgot, you're a demon. We don't have those here. You can't leave the apartment."

"And you can't leave me here without you. I'll burn while you're gone."

Damn. I forgot about that. I guess, somehow, I understood that I couldn't go too far from him inside of the apartment, but it never occurred to me that I can't go *outside* without him.

But I also really need my latte. I don't consider my caffeine addiction an addiction lightly. If I don't go down to The Beanery or even Dunkin', I'll still have to go to a store to buy some coffee for the apartment.

Either way, I gotta leave—which means that Mal has to come with me.

I huff, then give in. "Fine. But you have to turn into the mass of shadows. The one where I can't make out any of your features. No eyes. No horns. We can't let anyone see the real you."

It's not that I'm ashamed of being seen with the monster. It's more like I've spent nearly three decades in America. Can you imagine if the people who lived here with me discovered that demons existed?

No, thanks.

Turns out that doesn't seem to be a problem since Mal nods and says, "Yes. I know." Then, right in front of me, he goes from demon to the amorphous shadowy shape I mentioned before turning the opacity way down until he's barely there.

Wait—*what*? I'd been expecting an argument, and instead I got a surprise and a freaking magic trick.

I don't know why, but since he's so determined to get me to accept that I'm supposedly his "mate", I thought he would want to let everyone we met in on the secret. But he doesn't, and now I learn he has *another* form?

Shadow.

Demon.

Fire—though, thankfully, that only happened once.

And now, like, mist? It's excellent camouflage, at the very least.

This... this might work.

"When I'm with you, my Shannon, I can be myself. But I can control the shadows, going as dark or as pale as I need. How is this?"

"It's perfect, actually." I don't mind bringing him with me if he can do that. "And you won't switch, right? You'll stay out of sight?"

"I must," he says solemnly. "It is the duke's most fervent law. It's forbidden to let a mortal see us. If I do, I could end up in chains."

Oh. So it's not because of me, but because of the way things run back in his world. Hey. I'll take it.

"What about me?"

"You're my mate, Shannon. You are the only exception to the law. And even then…"

I wait a second to see if he's going to finish his statement. When he doesn't, I narrow my gaze on him. "Even then *what*?"

He bends slightly, folding his claws inward a split second before he gently strokes my cheek. "Nothing for you to worry about."

I want to argue. I want to stamp my feet and demand he tell me what happens if anyone sees him. I don't. I'm already feeling the beginnings of the headache I get if I don't get my morning caffeine, and considering how grave his tone was, I don't think he's going to risk breaking this duke guy's law.

"Fine. But behave yourself, okay?"

"Whatever you wish."

It's Sunday. The Beanery is open by seven, and Derek has the morning shift.

For the first time in weeks, though, I don't spend my walk to the coffee shop wondering if he'll be wearing the green polo that brings out his eyes or the white one that makes his tan pop. I'm completely consumed with making sure that no one notices that I have two shadows.

Beneath the sunlight, Mal can actually adjust how dark he appears as a shadow. The amorphous shape hides most of his demonic features, and his faded form stays within a few steps of me so that we don't risk his catching on fire out on the street. Unless someone was really paying close attention to me, they'd never notice the spare shadow—and I tell myself that the entire walk to The Beanery.

I almost went to Dunkin' instead. It's a little farther of a walk—about twelve blocks instead of six —and I was willing to risk being out longer if it meant that I didn't bring Mal to one of my regular haunts. Only then I remembered that I owed Derek the $4.50 from yesterday's second latte so The Beanery it was.

As soon as I reach the front door, I gauge the distance between the entrance and the counter. The Beanery is a cozy café. It's small enough that Mal should be fine waiting outside while I get my coffee.

"Stay here," I murmur to him. "I'll be right back."

A warm heat brushes against my arm. Mal. I'm gonna take that as a *yes*.

Exhaling softly, I grab the door, pulling it open.

"Shannon! Right on schedule," Derek says, waving at me. He finishes up with his last customer, passing over their pastry, then immediately reaches for the milk. "Can I get you anything with your latte?"

My plan had been to get my drink, pay Derek for yesterday, then go back to my apartment where I don't have to worry about Mal losing control of his shadow form in public.

But then it hits me. A spark of brilliance.

"Actually, yes."

"What do you need?"

"Kennedy's phone number."

Derek's friendly smile droops. "Excuse me? Kennedy… from next door?"

Okay. I can see how that sounds kind of weird. I should probably explain.

"Yeah. I stopped by yesterday and saw that she's still got the note about her vacation on the door. I have a question about a book I bought from her and… I don't know. You work here. She works there. I was wondering if maybe you had her number?" I say. "A last name, maybe? I really want to get in touch with her."

"Oh." Derek finishes making my latte, reaching for a lid. "So, it's about a book?"

I nod.

"Sorry. I'd give it to you if I did, but all I know is her coffee order. But, if you want, you can give me your number and if I see her before you do, I could let her know you want to talk to her."

"Yeah. Thanks." It's worth a shot. "I guess I could do that."

Derek presses a button on his register, shooting out a piece of receipt paper. After ripping it, he passes it to me, followed by a pen. I grab it, quickly jotting down my phone number, then hand it back.

He takes it, slipping it beneath the register till.

"If it's okay, maybe I could call it sometime, see if you're free to get dinner with me. I've been meaning to ask, but I guess I never got the chance until now. What do you say, Shannon?"

Last week, I would've been psyched that my barista boy was finally making a move on me. Heck, even yesterday morning, I would've jumped at the chance.

But now?

I don't dare look behind me. Mal's out there, and he still hasn't given up on this crazy idea that he's my mate. While I've come to believe that he'll never hurt me, I'm not so sure he'll be happy to hear another guy ask me out.

"Maybe," I say vaguely. "I… I've got a lot going on right now, but you never know, right?"

"Oh, sure. It's not like I don't see you all the time anyway. Just let me know."

If I sigh in relief, Derek might get the wrong idea. So, instead, I smile at him. "Sure. I'll do that."

With an answering grin, he puts my latte on the counter in front of me.

As he does, Derek glances over my shoulder. "Whoa. It just got real dark real quick. Are we supposed to be having an eclipse today or something?"

I spin to look.

Or something is right. Only it's not a sudden eclipse or an afternoon thunderstorm darkening the street outside of the coffee shop. It's a shadow.

Mal.

There's no doubt in my mind that it's him. It's barely ten o'clock in the morning, with the sun shining brightly. Unless there's a freak storm outside, there's only one thing that could cause such darkness.

Crap.

Reaching into my purse, I snatch my wallet. I quickly look through the bills I have in there, snagging a twenty. I press it into Derek's hand.

"For yesterday and today," I tell him, "plus a tip. Thanks, Derek. Bye!"

Before he can say anything about my sudden shift in mood, I throw my wallet back in my purse, grab my latte, then sprint for the door.

I haven't gotten confirmation that Mal is immortal yet, but I'm going to freaking kill him for this!

"Mal!" It's a harsh whisper as I burst out of The Beanery. "What part of 'don't let anyone see you' do you not understand?"

"It's isn't me, my Shannon," Mal says in a low voice.

It's coming from behind me. Of course it is. He must've followed me into The Beanery despite me telling him not to. On the plus side, he didn't draw anyone's attention to him during my chat with Derek.

Then again, that means the shadows in front of me don't belong to my demon.

"Well, if it's not you, then what the heck is that?" The shadows are growing thicker. Darker. Bigger. "Mal?"

"It's… I think it might be Duke Haures's soldiers."

What?

MALPHAS

I'd been expecting this.

I won't pretend like I hadn't hoped to mate Shannon to me by now. If she was a demoness, I would've bonded with her last night. But my mate is mortal, and I must follow her lead.

Even at the risk of angering the ruler of Sombra.

Unfortunately, I hadn't warned my mate about this. Mainly because I was so sure that I'd have wooed her and mated her long before Duke Haures sent his soldiers to drag me back to Sombra. I didn't want to push her. I wanted her to choose me because she recognized me as her male and not because our freedom was in jeopardy if I stayed in her world without a bond.

I could've released her. Grounding my teeth

together, dipping my horns in regret, I admit if only to myself that this wouldn't be happening if I'd accepted she didn't want me and I had released her from her mate's promise.

An honorable male would have.

I thought I was one. For my mate, I'll do anything.

Anything except give her up.

So maybe I'm not so honorable after all.

Her pointy little pale nose is scrunched up as she tilts her head back. She gapes at the shadows, stunned speechless, before she whirls on me.

"Duke?" she sputters. "*Soldiers?*"

If I wasn't so worried for her, I would think her even more adorable for her reaction.

I can't lie to her. It's not how a Sombra demon treats his mate. She deserves honesty, especially now that my selfishness has caught up to me.

"Yes. They've found me."

"Found you," squeals Shannon. "What do you mean *found you*? Who found you? What's going on?"

"There are rules," I admit with a heavy heart. Rules I knew well last night, and that I brushed past when my suspicious mate asked me about them. "The portal only opens between worlds to bring me to my mate if she's off-plane, and then when we're bonded and I want to bring her home with me. If this was Soleil… if this was Rouge Brille… it wouldn't matter. I could wait for you. But this is a mortal world. I wasn't supposed to stay."

She narrows her pretty blue eyes on me. "But you told me you couldn't go back unless I sent you back! Were you lying?"

Never.

What I told her… it was the truth. Unless I release her from her promise, I can't go more than a few steps away from her or else my essence will burn. But if I do? Or she accepts me as her mate? I can open a portal on my own without needing any of Shannon's magic.

For now, I can't create any which is why the duke is making one to get to me.

I shake my head to answer her, a quick jerk, keeping my attention on the gathering shadows. The duke must be very angry to risk his soldiers appearing where a human could see them. Whoever he sends will shift forms once they cross worlds, like how I went from my shadow form to my demon shape after Shannon summoned me to her side, but even if they fade away upon arrival, these shadows are certainly attracting attention.

The human male inside of her coffee shop had moved around the counter, watching the shadows with a curious expression before Shannon bolted for the door. I had wanted to linger, to warn the male that Shannon is mine, but once I realized what was causing the shadows, I had to follow her—and not only because I feared burning my essence again.

I'm not surprised she thought it was me losing

control. I almost did when I scented the lust pouring off of the human. He wanted my mate, even going so far as to offer to share a meal with her. If it wasn't for my giving my word to my Shannon back in her quarters, I might've risked breaking Duke Haures's laws by snarling a warning at my rival.

I didn't, but it doesn't matter now. He's sent his trackers after me even so, and once they discover that Shannon is my unbonded mate, they'll punish her, too.

Humans aren't supposed to know about demonkind. To reveal our existence is to court the duke's infamous wrath. I was allowed to show myself off to my mate, but once she refuted my claim— repeatedly—I knowingly stretched the bounds of Duke Haures's orders.

I wanted more time. In Sombra, we're allowed until the gold moon to finalize a mating before we have to release each other. If a mate can resist a bond in that time, Fate was wrong. Neither demon will ever have another mate, but they won't be tied together for life, either.

The human world is different. I peeked out of Shannon's window last night and saw that, in her realm, there's only one moon. It was a sliver hanging low in a dark sky, a glowing beacon that's nothing like the two moons in Sombra. In my realm, the main moon reflects red from Sombra's ash fields, and the gold moon rises once every cycle. As of last night, its cycle was closing in, but it wasn't over yet. I should've had more time.

There's only one thing I can think to do.

"The portal will be opening soon," I tell her.

"Should we run? You're fast. Why don't you pick me up and we can get the heck out before it does?"

If I wasn't so worried about facing any soldiers, I'd be pleased that my mate's first impulse is to leave *with* me instead of punting me into the open portal herself. And while I would love to have a chance to hold her in my arms, it wouldn't help.

"They're just as fast as I am, my mate," I say gently, "and they'd be able to follow my essence to your home anyway." Just like they tracked me to this point. "Unless…"

"Unless? *Unless* is good. What do we have to do?"

"If you let me give you my essence, it'll be harder for them to find me again. They'll be confused by what we create when our essences mingle together. Plus, I can hide you in my shadows once you have my essence. They'll see me, but they won't see you."

Even if I'm caught, Shannon will be safe. My shadows will protect her from the duke's soldiers if I can't find a way to escape punishment.

It's the only chance we have.

Shannon gives the portal another quick look. Because it's a rift built between worlds by Sombra mages millennia ago, it doesn't work as quickly as Shannon's spell had. The shadows have grown darker meaning our time is short, but she has a few moments to make up her mind.

"You're sure you're not just making this up so that I'll take your essence? Because, no offense, you wouldn't be the first guy who tried to dupe me into doing something I probably shouldn't."

"I won't say that taking my essence won't change you, my mate. It will. There are consequences to sharing essence without a complete bond. But like how you gave me the gift of your tongue when you gave me your essence, you'll know mine and be able to melt into my shadows."

Shannon nods, her fair hair falling forward to hide her pretty face. "And if I don't?"

"It's against the duke's laws for a human to learn about Sombra or face one of its demons. We'll be put in chains and punished since you're not fully my mate yet if he catches us."

"And if you hide me?"

"He won't come after you. And if I can explain why we're holding off on mating right away, he should leave me alone, too."

At least, I hope so.

"Then essence me up, Mal." She shoves her hand in front of me. "Chop, chop."

Since I already made my mate's promise to her the moment I first saw her, giving her my essence is as simple as laying my hand over one of her tiny ones. She jerks, hissing under her breath, but I don't remove my hand. I can't. To me, Shannon's white skin is icy cold, burning me the same way I'm sure my heated flesh does her. Once our essence is shared, our temperatures will change so that we're more compatible, but for now we have to bear it.

Seconds later, it's done. And a good thing, too, because right as I move in front of Shannon, wrapping her with my shadows, the portal opens.

Instantly, he goes from his demonic shape to faded shadows, the portal winking out behind him. I recognize him in the split second of his change, though.

Glaine.

Glaine is a wily demon, and one of Duke Haures's favored soldiers. The lord of Sombra would have only sent his best when he discovered that I crossed onto the human plane and didn't immediately bond Shannon to me as my mate.

"Twenty-five paces west," he says in Sombran. "Meet me in the shadows there, Malphas."

I can't refuse him.

Gesturing behind me for Shannon to stay close so that my shadows will continue to conceal her, I follow Glaine to a narrow strait between shops. It's closed on the far end, filled with refuse and stacks of boxes, but the overhanging roof lends enough shadow for Glaine to resume his darker shadowy form, complete with curved horns, glowing green eyes, and a scowl that has me gulping, grateful he can't sense my mate.

Following his lead, I revert to my shadow shape,

too. Anyone who glances down this path will see a darker shade of shadow and the glows of our eyes—mine yellow, Glaine's green—and that's all. If they come closer, they might notice our horns or the runes that linger on Glaine's arm from the spell that opened the portal for him, but we'll be gone before they get a better look.

Glaine nods at me, thick arms folded behind his back. "You know why I'm here, Malphas."

"I do."

"Duke Haures has made the law very clear. No Sombra demon is allowed to cross into a mortal world without his permission. This is a chain offense. You had to know that, too."

I did. Then again, that's only assuming I went off-plane on my own. I'm not sure if it makes any difference, especially since I haven't bonded my mate to me yet, but I have to get Glaine to understand.

"I didn't choose to come here. My mate summoned me."

"Yes, but you stand before me as an unmated male. Where is she then?"

She's behind me, but I'll never admit that to the soldier. "Waiting for me to return to her. She's a mortal. It takes time for her to understand what a mate bond truly means."

"You had a thousand years to find her, Malphas. And you expect me to believe that you did, but then you failed to mate her? Mortal or not, you're a Sombra demon. Your instincts are unmatched."

My instincts are, but so is how quickly my Shannon became the most important creature in *any* world to me.

"I have her mate's promise. Isn't that enough?"

Glaine looks down his long nose at me. "No. You have to finish your mating by the gold moon for it to be a true mating. Otherwise, you lose your mortal mate."

He has no idea how close to the truth he is.

"Tell Duke Haures that I will take as long as the gold moon if I must. I won't let any other humans see me, and none will know about Sombra. I just want time to prove to my mate that I'm hers."

"You better, otherwise it's chains."

Even worse, it's an eternity without my mate. "I understand."

Glaine lifts his hand. The runes stretching the length of his arm flare a bright golden shade, triggering the return portal. As soon as he lowers his hand, a portal appears in the depths of the shadows.

Without even a goodbye, the soldier disappears inside of it.

I exhale in relief. That went a lot better than I expected it to.

Once Glaine is gone, I give Shannon a signal. At the same time, I unravel the shadows that I built around her.

She takes three steps toward me, then smacks me on my forearm with her small fist. "A thousand years!" she says.

I wince. Even if Glaine didn't mention my age out loud, she would've known anyway from my essence. "Yes."

"A thousand years. You're a thousand years old, Mal!"

Actually, I'm halfway through my eleventh century, but I think it wiser not to clarify. I nod instead.

"Rob the cradle much? I'm fucking *twenty-nine*, dude."

"I know. But, you have to remember, that's in human years. In Sombra, times runs differently since we have so much of it."

In Sombra, while I longed for my mate, it *dragged*.

She scowls at me. "Don't try to justify it! Why didn't you tell me that you were so freaking old? And chains? What the hell? You go to jail if I don't put out? No." Her forehead furrows, her hand poking at it. "You get thrown in a dungeon." She glances up at me. "How the fuck did I know that?"

"Because you have my essence," I tell her. "And you know everything about me now."

Shannon blinks, dropping her hand. After a moment, she lets out a harsh breath. "Talk about freaking consequences," she mutters.

My poor mate. She has no idea.

SHANNON

Did I think it was bad enough when I summoned a shadow monster in my room and learned that he burns if I go too far away from him?

Yeah. That's nothing compared to the bomb dropped on me after I meet his buddy, Glaine.

Mal would point out that Glaine isn't his buddy; the green-eyed demon is an enforcer for the powerful Duke Haures, the ruler of Sombra. And I didn't actually *meet* him. Courtesy of Mal shielding me with his shadows, Glaine never even knew I was there as I eavesdropped on their little chat.

They spoke in Sombran, the harsh language that makes up the spells in my spellbook. I understood every freaking word of it, too, as if someone installed a translator chip in my mind or something. Like, I heard the foreign words, but I interpreted them as English in my head, so even though they weren't exact translations, I got the gist of it.

I brought Mal here with my spell. That triggered the mate bond he insists is between us, but Sombra demons aren't supposed to visit Earth. He could come here, claim me, go home, whatever, but if a human who *wasn't* his mate saw him, he's in deep shit.

I'm his mate. Whether he's mine is something totally different, but I've given up on arguing that fact with Mal. I kind of have to, since the whole "essence" swapping thing gave me an insight into the demon. He's absolutely convinced I'm his mate, his life's goal was to find me and wife me up, and he really did wait a thousand years so far.

Oh. Sorry. One thousand and forty-six years. Because, you guessed it, he's immortal.

And he's spent the first part of his never-ending life waiting for me. For little ol' Shannon Crewes. And if Mal's emotions can be trusted—and I can't see why they can't be because, yeah, he was telling the truth when he said he can't lie to me—I've lived up to his every expectation, and then some.

But that doesn't mean I'm going to tie myself to this demon that I literally just met *yesterday*.

To make matters worse, even if I did entertain this insanity, there's a deadline involved with Mal's trip to the human world. He has until the rise of the gold moon in Sombra to convince me to mate with him otherwise Glaine will return for him—and, this time, he'll bring the chains that both of the demons mentioned.

Great. So my choices are become a monster's mate, or be responsible for him going to demon jail.

I almost want to chuck the spellbook in my garbage disposal just to get out my frustrations about this situation.

It doesn't help that, when I mumble my options to Mal, he has to go all noble and assure me that, if he does end up in chains, the responsibility is all his. If he fails to show me why he's worthy of being my mate, he's the only one to blame for me refusing to accept his claim.

Which is true, but now that I can't be suspicious about whether what he says to me is bullshit or not, that just makes me feel guiltier.

Mal assures me that Glaine is gone. While I can instinctively sense where Mal is—thank you essence and your stupid "consequences"—I have no idea if the other shadow monster decided to stick around. To be on the safe side, I insist on going back to my apartment.

Of course Mal follows me. What else can he do? Light up Main Street?

Ugh.

After I let us into the apartment, I storm right to my bedroom. Mal's hot on my heels, still trying to apologize, while also going into detail about the ruler of Sombra, his laws, and what I should expect to happen next now that I've taken his essence inside of me.

I'm barely listening. I think I've got a handle on the consequences so far, and while suddenly knowing a demonic language is, not gonna lie, kind of cool, the way I'm so utterly aware of Mal has me feeling a bit itchy.

Brushing him off, I grab the spellbook. Part of me is still aboard the "feed the grimoire to my garbage disposal" train, while the rest realizes that I'll regret it later if I do. So, instead, I crack the book open, hoping that I can find the answers to questions I can't even pose right now.

The book is in Sombran. Mal gave me the gift of knowing his language. Maybe, now that I do, it'll help.

I start with the first page, glancing at the inner cover for no other reason than it's the first page. Nothing changes. It still says the book is called the *Grimoire du Sombra*, and it used to be owned by the missing Susanna M. Benoit.

I start to turn the page when, suddenly, I glance at the inner cover again.

This time, I look at the name under Susanna's delicate scrawl.

Amy. In a choppy children's handwriting, someone had written the name **AMY**. I'd initially disregarded it as a child Susanna had known who'd mimicked the scripted signature by trying to add their name directly beneath hers. I'm not so sure where I got that idea from, but it seemed to make sense when one of the articles about Susanna's disappearance mentioned her niece, Amelia.

Amelia.

Amy.

I frown, thinking it over. Susanna... she's been missing for more than thirty years. But what about Amy? Her name's in the book. At the very least, she would've been aware that it existed.

Could she possibly know more than that?

I grab my phone. Typing 'Amelia Benoit' into the search bar, I'm not holding out much hope that I'll actually find anything. Imagine my surprise when one of those old, abandoned social media sites flags as belonging to an Amelia "Amy" Benoit of Connecticut.

I jab the link, focusing on the name and the picture at the top of the page. The last entry was a sparkle .gif from April 2005, so I'm still figuring I'm wasting my time, until I notice something in her profile picture.

Wait a sec—

I click on it, blowing it up to fill my entire screen.

The picture of Amy shows a pretty chick around my age, if not a few years younger; makes sense since this is an old social media site. She has a round face with high, apple cheeks, a coy smile, and mahogany-colored hair that she has gathered together over her shoulder. Her head is tilted just enough to let the waves fall.

I zoom in a little further.

There.

Before yesterday, I never would've noticed the hazy shadow drifting right behind Amy. Shadows are shadows, right? But this one… it looks way too much like the wavy distortion of a faded Sombra demon sticking close by.

In case I'm imagining it, I hop off my bed, approaching Mal. Once I sat, he'd dropped down to my floor, purposely taking the spot in the center of the chalk pentacle instead of disappearing the portrait he made of me only this morning. As I rise, I see him begin to move, but I already expected it. His manners compel him to stand whenever I do, and while I appreciate the gesture, it's wasted on me.

"It's okay. Stay seated. I just want you to look at something. It's a photo on my phone." I shove it in front of him. "Do you see what I see?"

Mal squints at the screen. He's a little wary of my phone since they don't have anything like it in Sombra, but he focuses because he knows it's important to me.

I know the exact moment he sees what I did. His eyes light up as he whistles through his fangs.

That's what I thought.

"It's another demon, isn't it? A shadow monster, like you."

He nods. "A Sombra demon, yes. Or, at least, the essence of one who has marked this female as his mate."

And he's in the photo with the Amy Benoit who scrawled her name inside of the same spellbook that brought Mal here.

That, my friend, is what we call a lead. Feeling more hopeful than I have since I jokingly read the true love spell, I quickly select the option to PM this Amy. What are the odds that it'll reach her? Probably not good, but if she still has access to her email from twenty years ago, maybe she'll get it. If not, I'm going to keep searching for an updated way to contact Amy because, right now, it's the only thing I can think to do.

She might think I'm nuts for reaching out, or she might be the best shot I have to know what it's like to be a human involved with the demonic race.

Either way, I've got to try. And if Mal's expression stays thoughtful after I sit back down on the edge of my bed, that's fine.

Maybe he'd like to find out about that other demon, too.

CHAPTER 12
MATE SICKNESS

SHANNON

Two hours into my workday and I feel like absolute *garbage*.

On my best Mondays, it takes me past my morning coffee before I can act human. I usually hole myself up in my cubicle, checking my email and setting up my appointments for the week, before being sociable with my colleagues out in the break room.

I'm in sales. Technically, my title is account manager, but my job really revolves around selling office supplies in bulk. Real glamorous, I know. If you need a thousand paper clips and a box full of post-it notes, I'm your girl. These days, I get to make sure that our clients receive their orders on time as well as pushing them to add on reams of paper and pallets of toilet paper so our company can turn a profit off of theirs.

It is what it is. I earn a steady paycheck out of it, and it pays better than I ever would've guessed.

I almost called out this morning. I woke up feeling a little off, and lord knows I've banked more than enough PTO for a month's worth of sick days. Besides, having an unexpected demon for a house guest seemed like a good reason to play hooky, especially since the alternative was bringing him with me to the office.

In the end, I decided I wasn't feeling *that* bad. I had a couple of important meetings today that I'd rather not postpone, and I know now that I can trust Mal not to appear around any of my co-workers. If he does, that duke of his will somehow know and send his pitbull of a soldier after Mal. Since he doesn't want to cut short any of our time between now and the gold moon deadline, he'll be on his best behavior.

If only I was, too.

It starts with sweat forming along my brow. I almost feel feverish, and when I use the front-facing camera on my phone, I see that I'm flushed. My skin feels oversensitive, too. Even sitting in my office chair has me twitching until I get up and pace outside of my cramped cubicle for a few minutes.

My boobs ache. My stomach is tight. My head is throbbing, and, I kid you not, it feels like my damn clit is pulsing in time to my headache.

Something's wrong. By the time the nausea washes over me, I get up from my desk, dashing down the hall, aiming for the communal bathrooms on my floor.

I don't even remember the demon in that moment. All morning, Mal's been huddled under my desk, hiding in the shadows there. Close enough that he won't catch on fire, but out of sight from my co-workers.

Until I'm about to hurl and I just run.

Luckily, he comes after me. In his faded form, more of a shimmer than a true shadow, Mal is hot on my heels.

Because I can sense him there even if I can't see him, I leave the door open just long enough to let his shadows slip in ahead of me before I slam the door shut. There are three stalls in this bathroom. I do a quick check to make sure I'm alone—well, except for my shadow monster—then dash back to the door, locking it.

As soon as I do, Mal materializes fully. He skips right past his inky black shadow form, going fully demon. Good thing there's no cameras in here.

"Shannon." Concern laces his gravelly tone. "What's wrong?"

I wish I freaking knew.

When I bolted for the bathroom, I'd been aiming to reach the toilet in time. The urge to throw up has subsided some, but the rest of my symptoms have actually grown *worse*.

In a clipped voice in case I feel puke-y again, I quickly explain how shitty I feel to Mal. I doubt he'll be able to help me—what does he know about human illnesses, right?—but, to my shock, he nods along as I speak.

"It's the mate sickness," murmurs Mal when I'm done. "I should've known."

"Mate sickness?" I echo. Oh, *heck* no. "What do you mean, mate sickness? How do I cure it?"

Instead of explaining what it means, he simply says, "I have to touch you."

I glare at Mal. "Touch me? Okay. What does *that* mean?"

"Your body needs mine."

"How fortunate," I snap. "I get some weird demon sickness and the only cure is your dick, is that it?"

Mal frowns. "I warned you there would be consequences of you accepting my essence."

Are you kidding me? "You said consequences, Mal. You didn't tell me that this was a way to trick me into mating you."

"What?" His eyes go wide as though he finally understands what I'm implying. "Shannon, no. It's not like that. Yes, you having my essence inside of you will make you more susceptible to our mate bond, but you don't have to do anything you don't want to. I meant it when I said I just had to touch you. It doesn't mean intimately. Here." He holds out his hand. "Touch me. See if that helps."

I want to believe he's full of it. Maybe if I didn't feel like I was on fire myself, I would. Still glaring at him, I snatch his hand. Considering it's so much bigger than mine, the most I can do is wrap my fingers around two of his, but I do it.

And immediately feel ten degrees cooler.

The nausea? Gone.

Damn it.

I give it a few seconds, then drop his hand. "Is that enough? Will this 'mate sickness' go away now?"

Mal swallows roughly. I know then that whatever he's going to say next, I won't want to hear it.

"You're still getting used to my essence. It might go away for a little bit, or I might have to touch you some more."

I narrow my gaze. "Touch me *how*?"

"I won't lie to you, Shannon. An intimate touch is best, but we don't have to do that. Just a caress whenever you're feeling needy should be enough."

"A caress?" I ask. From a monster no one else is allowed to see. "Where?"

In answer, Mal moves into me. "How's this?" He runs the side of his claw along the edge of my jaw before tracing it up my cheek. "Better?"

A shudder runs down my spine. If touching his

hand gave me some relief, that charged touch knocked out half of my sickness with a single stroke.

"*Yes.*"

I get it now. With my body urging me to find pleasure with Mal's because of this unfinished mate bond and the way we swapped our essence, the more sexual the touch, the better I'll feel.

If his gentle touch against my jaw and my cheek feels that amazing, what if…

"I don't want to mate," I tell him, making sure that I'm perfectly clear. If I'm going to go through with this, I want to set my boundaries. "No fucking, but I can't spend the rest of the day sick like this. I also can't disappear into the bathroom so you can touch me without my colleagues beginning to think I've got the runs. But if your touch helps me that much, what do you think an orgasm will do?"

Oh. Look at that. I've stunned Mal speechless.

Big guy's mouth is hanging open and everything.

I quirk my eyebrow. If I wasn't so serious about this, I might actually find his reaction kind of funny. "Well?"

He clears his throat. "Are you asking me to give you pleasure?"

If I could get myself off, I wouldn't be asking him. Something tells me, though, that I'll only get sicker if I try.

In answer to his question, I unbutton my pants, then tug on the zipper. It echoes in the bathroom. Mal doesn't even blink as I slowly shimmy my work pants down to my knees, then yank my panties next.

"Only if you want to, but I'm down. I want you to make me feel good, Mal," I tell him. "To make this sickness go away."

Mal lifts his hands, looking at his fingers as if he's never seen them before. After a few seconds where I'm beginning to feel like an idiot with my pants down, he shakes his hands. When he's done, most of his hands are still the deep red of his demonic form. The tips of his fingers all the way to his claws, though? They're turned to shadow.

"So I don't scratch you with my claws," he says by way of explanation. "Shannon… you really want me to do this?"

Do I really want him to finger me until I come in the bathroom? "I can't be sick all day," I repeat.

That's all the permission he needs. Tucking me against him, my back to his chest, Mal bows over my body, tentatively touching my throbbing pussy. I didn't realize just how hot and horny I was until I yanked down my panties and noticed the damp spot.

Freaking hell, I'm soaking wet.

Mal lets out a murmur of appreciation when he realizes the same thing.

"You're so warm. So slick." He runs his finger along my slit before finding my opening. "I never knew a cunt could be like this."

I sputter. Turned on and melting against him,

hearing him call my pussy a cunt like that—so raw, so possessive—is like a needle scratching on a record. Everything stops, and all I can do is swivel my head, looking up at him.

Mal's gaze has gone heavy-lidded. His golden eyes are brighter than I've seen before, swallowing the sliver of his pupil. Soft breaths pant out through his slightly parted lips. I can feel the rise and fall of his chest behind me, the curve of his arms reaching around me. With his big body contorted to cover me, he's nearly bent in half in order for him to reach my pussy.

I go up on my tip-toes, making it a little easier for him.

He runs his blunt finger up the length of my slit again, shuddering when he lifts his hand and sees the slick moisture he collected. If I wasn't feeling so hot and achy, I might've been shocked by the way he licks his finger clean, murmuring, "Delicious," in his impossibly deep voice. As it is, I'm just wishing he'd put his finger back.

Luckily, my demon obliges.

Mal buries that same finger between my folds, learning my most intimate places as he touches me *everywhere*. I lean against him, his big body bracing my back, as he nudges my swollen clit, but when he slides down and finds the opening to my pussy again, I can't help it.

I shift, moving just enough to entice him to dip his

finger inside of me. He pauses when I take the tip, but when I try to lean back, forcing him to go a little deeper, Mal follows my lead and goes at least a knuckle deep.

I need *more*.

"Oh." I throw my head back, leaning against his muscled torso. "That. Do that again."

He does.

Damn it, but he plays my body like a freaking fiddle. Instead of plucking strings, he dips his finger inside of me, stroking me leisurely before picking up the pace. His fingers are thick enough that it feels more like a cock inside of me, and wanton that I am, you know I start riding him.

With his other hand, he pays firm attention to my clit. Rubbing it, circling it, even tapping it, he stimu-lates it to the point that I'm on the verge of coming. With his first few knuckles lodged firmly inside of me, giving me something to clench, I explode in his arms.

Just as I let out a sharp shriek to let him know I've climaxed, I turn and bury my face in Mal's bare chest. Here's hoping I didn't scare my office the way I did Mrs. Winslow because, yup, I'm a screamer.

Finally, I collapse against him. I'm as weak as a kitten after that, and I barely know what Mal is doing until he's maneuvered my lower body, gently easing my work pants, then my panties off of my body. I'm naked from the waist down, except for my heels, and I begin to realize that this might not be a good idea.

Forget the fact that he's pleasuring me inside of my work bathroom. If he whips out his cock and tries to shove it inside of me, I... I might just let him.

Not good, Shannon. I come back to reality just in time to push away from Mal.

He retaliates by gripping my waist securely in his big hands.

"Mal, what are you— *whoa*."

He doesn't do anything about his own shadow-based clothing. Instead, he steals a quick kiss that has me blinking up at him. Next thing I know, he's lifting me off of the ground, settling me on top of the nearest sink.

"Mal!" I squeal. The porcelain is chilly and it's a shock against my bare ass. As overheated as I am, it feels like I'm sitting on a block of ice instead of a sink. "Put me down."

"I have, my mate. I've put you down right where I want you."

He lowers his big body to his knees. With me on the counter and Mal kneeling before me, his mouth is on the level of my pussy.

I should've known then what he was thinking, but I'm still trying to get over how hard he made me come from just his finger.

"Grab my horns," he growls, tilting his head toward me so that they're within my reach, "and hold tight."

I scooch forward, gripping his horns like they're a steering wheel. "Like this?"

"Unh—*yes*."

I already let him finger me to an orgasm. He wasn't wrong when he said that his touch would ease the sickness I was suffering from, and I've gone from feeling like I was going to hurl, to thinking I would die if he didn't let me come on his hand. Now I want him to do it again, and this way, I can actually open my legs wider, giving him easier access.

Mal obviously has other plans. Instead of using this new position to bring me closer to his hand, the big demon moves closer to me until his mouth is inches away from my sensitized pussy.

"I must taste this cunt, my Shannon," he pants out, his excitement making his breaths come quickly. Warm air bathes my pussy, tickling my damp curls. "Don't deny me."

As if I freaking could?

I open my mouth if only to tell him not to call my pussy a cunt when Mal darts out his tongue. Just like he knew that I wanted to kiss him, he has to be able to tell that he totally has my permission to, uh, taste me.

And taste me he does. Mal starts with a few delicate flicks of his tongue, purposely avoiding my throbbing clit as if he can sense I'm seconds away from going off like a rocket. He already made me come once, and I'm ready to do it again within a few licks. Too bad Mal wants to freaking torture me. His licks become longer, harder, rougher. His thumbs dig into my thighs as he keeps me perched on the edge of the sink while he takes hold of one of my labia, sucking it into his hot mouth.

It feels fucking *amazing*.

"Mal…" I tilt my hips, trying to grind myself against his face. The horn makes it easy for me to steer him exactly where I want him, and his wide face gives me plenty of room to move against so that I hit the right spot. When I do, I can't help but groan. "Oh, god, *yes*."

His chuckle sends vibrations all the way through me. Barely taking his mouth away from my flesh, he says, "I'm glad you're pleased, my mate," before he dives back in, paying dedicated attention to my clit.

I'm so close I *hurt*. I'm not sure I can take much more stimulation, and as the beginning of another orgasm starts building low in my gut, I try to scoot away from him.

Mal doesn't let me.

He's too strong. Even as I kick him in the side, he's single-mindedly devoted to tearing another climax out of me.

And he does.

Letting go of his right horn, I shove my hand inside of my mouth, muffling my scream in time for it to rip out of me.

My legs quake, but Mal holds them tightly in

place, keeping me secure on the edge of the sink as he nuzzles my clit with his cheek.

"Uxor mi," he whispers into my thigh. He's slipped back into Sombran, but like he knows my language now, I know his. "Fiore mi. Shannon mi."

Uxor mi. Fiore mi.

My mate. My flower.

My Shannon.

CHAPTER 13
HOME

SHANNON

When I finally come down enough to speak, the first thing I say is, "We can't do that again."

Even as I'm putting as much force behind it as humanly possible, I know I'm full of it. Mal's touch might be enough to cool the fire raging inside of me, but now that I've experienced what it's like to have his fingers stroking my clit, his mouth nuzzling me as he eats me out like I'm his favorite meal and he's freaking *starving*… if he offers to go down on me, I don't know if I'm strong enough to refuse.

That's why I tell Mal we can't. If I've learned anything after taking his essence from him, it's that he'll respect my wishes. He'll do what I say.

And if I lay back, spread my legs, and tell him to go to town, he won't hesitate to pleasure me.

This is insane. I've had lovers who treated giving me head like a chore to get through so that they can convince me I owe them. That it's up to me to return the favor. I've had others who refused to put their mouth down there, even though they had no problem trying to stick their cock in any hole I had.

But Mal... he treated the act like a reward. His gentle touch was at odds with how ravenously he licked and sucked me, reveling in my scent as he instructed me to hold on tight to his horns. I might have the imprint of the sink in my ass for the next few hours, and I don't know how long it's going to take until I get feeling back in my shaky legs, but I've never come so freaking hard in my life.

On the plus side, I don't feel sick anymore. And if the endorphins rushing through me right now are enough to keep it at bay, I might not have to be intimate with Mal again.

He's still hovering, his hands squeezing my thighs as if he's thinking about keeping me pinned there so he can dive back into my pussy. The way he licks his lips before dabbing the edge of his fang with his tongue makes me sure of it.

I... I kind of forgot about those fangs. I was so out of my head with lust that I eagerly let a fanged demon put his sharp canines near my lady bits. He didn't hurt me—unless you count how much pleasure he gave me—and, despite the way he acted like mine was the first pussy he ever touched, I can't fight the suspicion that he's had a lot of practice going down on women to make sure he could lick and suck without a single bite. Then there was his little trick with his claws…

And, no, the idea that he might have done that countless times over the last thousand years doesn't bother me at all. Why do you ask?

I nudge him with the tip of my high heel. Somehow I didn't lose my shoe the whole time I writhed on the sink. My clothes, however, are a different story. I've got to find them.

"Move. I want to get down."

Mal immediately steps back. But, before I can hop down, he lashes out his hands, grabbing me by the waist again. Without any effort at all, he lifts me up from the edge of the sink, setting me down on my feet.

I huff. "Could've done that myself, you know, but thanks, I guess."

"You're still not completely well, my mate," he says. Considering his mouth is wet from my latest orgasm, I decide to give him a pass when he calls me his mate. "Let me steady you."

I throw my hand out, trying to keep *some* space between us. "I'm fine."

Mal grabs my hand, taking it in his. Using the same finger that had been inside of me, Mal gently strokes the bite mark that decorates the fleshy part of my palm between my thumb and my pointer finger.

"Does it hurt?"

My first instinct is to yank my hand back. It messes with my head that he can be so merciless with my body one second, then this sweet and caring next. If he keeps tending to me like this, I might forget that he is only doing all of this because he thinks of me as his own personal pussy.

Mal calls me his mate, but I know better. *Fated schmated*. I'm the idiot who didn't figure out how to banish him after I unwittingly summoned him into my bedroom. I let him kiss me, then I let him go down on me. And let's not forget the whole "sharing essence" thing that got me into this mess in the first place.

Consequences, he said. I guess I never expected that giving him permission to shield me in his shadows meant that I'd grow desperate for his touch.

Because that's exactly what happened. At least I'm better now.

"Told you," I said, moving around him, gathering up my panties and my work pants. "I'm fine."

I shake out my pants. Damn it! They're all wrinkly now. Scowling, I yank on my underwear, then start to shimmy on my pants just in time for someone to start rattling the locked door to the bathroom.

Crap. How long have we been in here? So consumed by what Mal was doing to my body, it could've been hours; it wasn't, but it was at least a good ten minutes. Of course someone would have to use the communal bathroom eventually, and I locked the freaking door.

I whirl on Mal. Smart demon. He's already transformed into the softest of shadows. If I didn't know he was here, I never would've noticed him tucked beneath the sink we so unceremoniously christened.

Hurriedly yanking my zipper, I pull the edge of my blouse down to hide the fact that I didn't have the chance to button up my pants. "Coming!"

Mal chuckles. I wince. My voice is raw and throaty, and my word choice? Yeah. Not the best.

"Shannon? Is that you? Are you in there?"

Lisa. My boss.

Oh, come *on*.

I clear my throat. "Yes. Sorry… give me a sec."

Dashing forward, wobbling on my heels, I unlock the door before throwing it open.

Lisa is a motherly woman in her late fifties. She has a rounded face, salt-and-pepper hair that she wears to her chin, and wide dark eyes. Right now, they're filled with concern as she looks me over.

"How are you? Chris told me that you weren't feeling so well."

I can only imagine what I look like. My cheeks have got to be flushed again, and my legs are still feeling pretty weak after how hard Mal made me come. The blonde flyaways that frame my face are plastered to my forehead and my temples. Before, I was sweaty and sick; now, I'm breathing shallowly as I recover from my last climax and the nerves surrounding my boss checking me out on the heels of my monster pleasuring me.

"I'm not. I'm feeling kinda queasy."

And that is one hundred percent the truth.

She frowns. "Forgive me for saying so, but you don't look so great."

Don't feel so well, either.

"I should be getting better—" I begin, but Lisa cuts me off with a firm shake of her head.

"No, no. This is what we have PTO for. I can't have one of my best account managers fighting through the day. Clear your schedule and go home, Shannon. Get some rest. Feel better."

I open my mouth to argue again, but then I realize something. Lisa is right. I never take PTO; in fact, during my end-of-year reviews, she's always on my case about making sure I do so I don't get burned out. She's my boss, and I never forget she works for our company the same way I do, but she's a pretty decent lady. If she thinks I should take the day off, maybe I should.

I can tell that I'm not going to be able to argue with her anyway. And it's not like I have anything scheduled for the rest of the day that I can't miss. I did push through the two most important meetings I had already before running into Chris in the break room. He'd pointed out I didn't look so hot then, and I guess he passed the message along to Lisa when he saw her.

Probably shouldn't have dashed by his desk, calling out, "I'm gonna hurl," too, huh?

"Thanks, Lisa. I… I'll try."

WHILE I LIKE TO WALK AROUND MAIN STREET, AND my apartment building is on Calvert, just off of Main, I work on the other side of Jericho. I drive there and back every day.

They don't have cars in Sombra. When the shadow-based race of demons can basically fly, there's no need for such mundane travel. I'd gotten a kick out of the ride into work this morning because Mal kept marveling over something I obviously take for granted. He dissolved into shadows, hovering over my passenger seat, in awe of how fast the car went, and all the different colors he saw as we passed through the more forested side of the city.

We're both still humming on the way back to my apartment. Proving that he might just know me better than I want to admit, Mal stays quiet. As much as he can, he gives me space, and if my small coupe is filled with heat as we both relive what we did in the bathroom, I fix that by blasting my AC.

After he gave me his essence, I'd grown more used

to his temperature. Another one of those consequences, I guess. He's not as boiling to the touch as he
was, and I'm not burning up myself anymore, but my
car's air conditioner is definitely a godsend during the
twenty-minute ride back to my apartment.

I learn there's another "consequence" besides the
supernatural level of horniness I experienced earlier.
When I ran for the bathroom, there was a moment
between me bolting and Mal chasing after me where I
went just past the length of the bond between us.
Whether I want to admit it's there or not doesn't
matter when Mal goes up in flames when I get too far
for him.

But I did, and he didn't, and it turns out that him
giving his essence means that we can have a little
more space. Of course, he tells me that after I learn I
might feel sick again without his touch, so it's not like
he's going anywhere.

Yay, Shannon.

At least I'm not sick now. Actually, now that I've
gotten over the mate sickness, I'm pretty hungry. I
stop at the only drive-thru that is between my job and
my apartment, ordering way too much food. Over the
last two days, I've discovered that Mal has quite the
appetite. Calling this lunch, I get one of every type of
sandwich for the demon to try, plus a combo for me.

Hey. So long as I'm stuck with him, I gotta feed
him, right?

Because I don't want anyone in the parking lot to

wonder why the bags of food are floating on their own, I insist on carrying them. Mal offers anyway, pointing out that the parking lot is empty when I pull in—because, duh, it's almost noon on a freaking Monday—but I can't risk it.

I lower the window enough for him to get out of the car. Once he has, I raise it again, then kill the engine.

Climbing out, grabbing the food, I turn to Mal. "Ready— wait. Where did you go?"

Because he's not next to me right now.

I squint. I'm getting better at picking up Mal's faded shadow and I follow it across the parking lot, my heels *click*-ing against the asphalt in time to find Mal crouched behind the dumpster.

What the…

With the shadows back there being so dark, he's shifted his form to match them. He's in his inky black shadowy form, the one where I can pick out his horns, his arms, his legs. Unlike how they disappear as he fades, his eyes are shining brightly as he reaches out his hand.

"Mal?"

"It's alright, wee creature," he coos. "I will help you."

It's hard for me to look around his bulk. I have no idea what he's doing, but when I hear a frightened *squeak*, I jump back, tottering on my high heels— especially when Mal slips his shadowy hand in the gap between the dumpster and the asphalt beneath it.

I swear to God, if he picks up a rat, I'm so out of here.

"There you are. I've got you."

But it's not a rat. When he turns around, revealing what he has cradled in his palm, I see that it's a kitten with downy black fur and filmy eyes. They're open, so it's not a really young kitten, though it's definitely too small to be on its own.

The kitten lets out a soft *mew*. Almost immediately, a larger, sleek black cat comes racing out from beneath one of the parked cars. Her ears are twitching, searching for the kitten, and she makes a bee-line for the shadows.

She must've been watching the dumpster, waiting for her kitten to find its way back out since she was far too big to get the kitten herself.

When the cat stops a good couple of feet away from Mal, obviously intrigued by the shadow monster who has her kitten, he rises up from his crouch before slowly lowering his hand.

He sets the kitten down in front of the mama cat, then backs up. "This must be yours."

The cat darts forward, sniffing her baby. Once she's assured herself that the kitten is unharmed, she grips the kitten's scruff gently between her fangs. But, instead of bolting like I expect, she actually moves closer to Mal, rubbing her flank alongside his muscular calf before she finally does take off with her baby.

He brushes his hands together, glancing over at me. "What is it, my mate?"

I'm staring. I know I am. "Didn't take you for a cat whisperer."

"Is that what the creature is called? A cat?"

I nod.

He mulls that over for a moment. "Was I supposed to whisper? I kept my voice low so I didn't frighten the baby cat, but I don't think it was a whisper."

Sometimes I forget that Mal's knowledge of English isn't a direct translation, just like the way I understand Sombran more as vibes than actual text.

Shaking my head, I say, "You did fine. I mean, you saved the kitten. The baby cat," I explain. "But… how did you know it was in trouble?"

"I heard the squeaks of distress when I left the car. I couldn't leave it there. It was frightened." He turns his head slightly, eyes following the path the mother cat had taken. "I know what it's like to feel trapped."

Right. Because I summoned him and left him in a salt circle.

Turning back to me, Mal's expression has softened. "All it takes is someone who cares enough to free you."

Oh. *Oh.*

He means me, doesn't he?

I don't know what to say. I'm still stunned by how kind he was to that kitten, and how unexpectedly touched that left me feeling.

Touched—and a little turned on.

Okay. A *lot*.

He meets my gaze. Breathing in deep, his nostrils flare as his golden eyes shine bright.

The next thing I know, he's standing in front of me, his big hand extended.

"Come, my mate. Let's go home."

I want to point out just how dirty it sounds when Mal rasps out 'come' like that. I want to remind him that this is *my* home, and once I figure out how to open a portal on my own, he'll be going back to his.

But I don't.

I place my hand in his. "Sure. Why not?"

CHAPTER 14
PLEASURE

MALPHAS

As delicious as the meat patties Shannon bought for me are, nothing makes my mouth water more than the taste of my mate's cunt.

I knew that the mate sickness would eventually find her. With our essences shared, and our mate's promises unfulfilled, the bond stretching between us would compel her to seek out my touch. I've had a thousand years to get used to the ache of being without my female, and I've been battling my need since I first took Shannon's essence inside of me. She was unprepared for how it would affect her, and it was awful watching her suffer when I would do anything to ease her.

Did I expect to be given the honor of placing my

153

mouth against her cunt? *Never.* As strong and as stubborn as she is, I thought Shannon would be able to deny the mate sickness the same way she openly denies the lust she feels for me. After how I angered her by stealing the kiss she wanted, I vowed I would never take anything from my mate that she didn't offer freely first.

Just a brush of my finger would be enough to soothe the sickness. I made sure she understood that —and still she undressed, opening up her body to my hands, then my mouth.

Of course, she regretted it. Why wouldn't she? I had told her there would be consequences, but I'm still that selfish male who didn't go far enough to explain what they might be. I knew that she only let me touch her because it was a better option than suffering the mate sickness.

And while there was no denying that, when Shannon grabs me by my finger, leading me to her bedroom even before she unpacks the human food, she's not sick when she asks me if I'm interested in touching her again.

I have her coverings off and her legs thrown over my shoulders before she can even think to change her mind.

To my absolute amazement, for the rest of that day, then the one following it, my Shannon is keen to allow me to pleasure her body. Has a male ever been as lucky as I am? She invites me to slip my finger inside of her warm cunt, feasting on it to gather up all of the physical essence that gathers there, while also revealing her breasts to me. As bountiful as they are without any kind of covering, they're a perfect handful for me, and I discover my Shannon loves it when I knead the mounds before slipping her pebbled nipples between my lips.

It isn't long before there isn't a single inch of her that I haven't branded with my touch. I live to make her come, to hear her squeal in pleasure, and when she shoves me away because she's had enough, she lets me explore the art she has on her body.

My beautiful mate is covered in flowers. I love them, though I always end up tracing the sunflower etched on her arm.

Blooms in the sun… full of magic…

Mate.

Mine.

She's fond of me. Though our bond is barely a thread stretching between us, I know my Shannon intimately—and I don't just mean her luscious body. I know she cares. If I was a human male, one she didn't have to hide, I have no doubt that she wouldn't continue to deny the path Fate set out for us.

I can't blame her, though. Our differences aren't too much for me to overcome, but Shannon has a harder time with the idea that she belongs to a Sombra demon. And while she lets me pleasure her body, until I have her heart and her soul, it's not enough.

I keep trying. I do everything I can to prove that I will be the perfect mate for her. I feed her. I clothe her. She is my muse, and my light. And even if the gold moon comes and she refuses me, I'll still treasure the time we shared together.

Especially when she makes it so that we have even more.

The morning after my first taste of her, I expect her to wake up and tell me that we're going back to that tall building with her cramped workstation. Unlike my easel and my paints, her tools include a bigger version of her glass box—she calls one a tablet, the other her phone—and a box that makes a soft whine. A row of buttons that go *click-clack* every time she hits one with her fingers is attached to the box, and when I asked her if this is her TV since it looks like the one she pointed out in her home, she said it was a computer, then hushed me so that her fellow humans couldn't hear me.

She guards me against Duke Haures's wrath almost as fiercely as I will forever protect her.

I love her. I've loved her from the moment I felt our bond awaken, everything that Shannon was and will be filling the emptiness in my chest. I stroke her with the reverence owed a goddess, and I wait anxiously for the scent of her lust to perfume the air. Whenever it does, I know that she will crook her finger and I'll find my fondest treasure between her thighs.

It's been two full days since my insatiable mate gave me the honor of being the male to slake her lust. I keep expecting her to decide that she's had enough, that the mate sickness has no sway over her, but that doesn't happen.

In fact, on the third afternoon that Shannon stays in her quarters with me, she calls me to her bedroom. I eagerly join her, surprised when she's still completely clothed. When my mate hungers for my touch, she immediately begins to undress.

But not now.

"My Shannon? Did you need me?"

I take a tentative sniff. Though I spend my nights watching over her from my perch on the floor, she allows me to pleasure her on her bed. I smell her musk mingling with the essence I can't control; beneath my shadow coverings, I often erupt in time with my mate's climaxes. Her lust overlays the scents of her previous pleasure. It's fresh, but still she stays covered.

She nods, her pretty blue eyes almost cloudy with need. Nibbling her bottom lip with her tiny human teeth, she gestures to the shadows concealing my cock from her.

"If I asked you to, would you get rid of those shadows for me?"

I stop breathing. My mate... surely she's not asking me to bare myself to her?

Gulping, I say, "Whatever you wish."

"Okay." Shannon nods. "I... I kinda want to see it."

It. My cock. I'm in a constant state of arousal around my mate, the mate sickness affecting me in other ways, and I know what she'll see if I do that.

But she asked, and I can deny my mate nothing.

With a wave of my hand, the coverings are gone.

"Okay. It's... it's bigger than I remember, but okay." She nods, more to herself than to me. "Question for you. That trick of yours..."

"Trick?" I repeat. I don't understand. "What trick?"

"You know." Shannon wiggles her fingers at me.

I'm perplexed. "I'm sorry, my mate. But I have no idea what you're talking about."

She huffs. "Come on, Mal. That thing you do where you're solid for the most part, but there are other things on you that are shadowy. Like what you do when you..."

Ah. "When I pet your cu—"

"Pussy," Shannon quickly cuts in. "Let's get that straight. You have a cock and I have a pussy, and that's what we can call them, okay?"

I frown. In her language, pussy also refers to that little creature I found mewing in the shadows. While 'cunt' is the closest translation to the Sombran word for her sex, I can see why Shannon calls her genitals her 'pussy'. When I lick her, she certainly mewls like that wee furry beast I rescued.

"Yes," I agree. It's such a small request, and I'm eager to prove to my mate that there isn't anything— no matter how tiny—that I won't do for her. "As for my claws, I didn't want to stab you with them when I was petting your pussy."

"Can you do that with your dick? Make it easier for me to… handle?"

Sweat starts to bead along my brow. My sack is already heavy.

"Yes." It's a harsh rasp. "If my mate wishes it, I can."

I do. It takes a lot of control for a Sombra demon to only transform along the edges, but I've always been able to. With only a bit of focus—which, I admit, is a little harder than usual at the moment—I can make my cock more proportionate to her hand.

Her eyes light up. "Oh. That… that's exactly what I was hoping for. Wait…"

Wait? No. I don't think I can.

But I must. "Of course."

She shakes her head as if I've gotten the wrong idea somewhere. "I can feel your shadow like a breeze on my skin. What about you? Can you feel me? If I touch you when you're shadow?"

Does that mean she wants to touch my cock?

Moisture beads at the tip. If I don't get control of

myself, just Shannon's curious questions will have me exploding before she even puts her hands on me.

I nod my head. It's the most I can do right now.

She steps into me. Her hand is within inches of my aching erection.

"Can I?" she whispers. "Touch you, I mean?"

My hands curl of their own accord. I fist them completely, tucking them behind me so that I don't frighten her away.

I nod.

Shannon reaches out, laying her fingers along my shaft. When I jolt at the supreme pleasure I feel from that single touch, she grows bolder. With my cock half demon, half shadow, she's able to close her fingers around the width.

Starting at the base of my shaft, she gives me a quick stroke.

And I lose it.

My instincts take over. Wrapping one arm around Shannon, I heft her off the ground, groaning in relief when my mate doesn't release her grip on my cock. I fly across the room with her, backing her against her wall, letting go in time to brace my huge body over her slight mortal form.

I don't want to hurt her. It's easy to remember my strength when I'm worshiping her body, but when she tends to mine, I'm afraid I'll lose control further. This way, I can jab my claws in the wall instead of her, bellowing my pleasure against my forearm instead of roaring for her human neighbors to hear.

Shannon laughs. It's such a sweet sound, all the sweeter for how she's resumed her stroking. "If you wanted me to stroke you off over here, Mal, you could've said."

Lowering my chin so that it's pressed to the side of her head, I rasp, "Is that what you're doing? Stroking me off?"

She gives me an impish shrug. "Figured it was your turn."

I stiffen, and not just my throbbing cock. Straightening up, I begin to pull away from her. "There are no turns. I pleasure you because I need to. And you —*unh*."

She squeezed my cock. I almost climax then and there, and when she tugs me by my shaft, it's even harder to hold back.

"Get it through your thick skull," she says, her tone teasing though the room is heavy with our combined lusts, "I'm doing this because I want to. If you rather I didn't, that's fine. Just tell me no."

I don't. I can't.

Shannon strokes me again. "See? Don't fight with me, big guy. I know what I want. And, no matter what happens next, I'd kick myself forever if I didn't get to play with you just once. So hold onto the wall, be quiet, and let me have some fun."

"As… as you wish."

SHANNON

Mal is breathing heavily.

Bracing one hand against the wall, claws digging into the sheetrock, his other hand is fisted at his side. It didn't take much to make him go off. His come is spattered against the hem of my t-shirt, both of my palms, and when I turn to glance behind me, I see he even managed to get an arc of the thick, white fluid to hit the lower part of the wall. Between that and the claw marks, I'm going to have to worry about damage control if I keep my monster.

I blink. *Keep* him? Where did *that* thought come from? And why does it not freak me out as much now as it did the other day in the shadows when I found out that either I mate Mal before the gold moon or I lose him?

I shake my head, knocking my loose hair back with a sticky hand.

As I do, I start to slide out from beneath the cage of his body. When he first grabbed me, I wondered if I made a huge mistake, deciding to take his monster cock on for size. When I discovered that he could actually shrink his dick so that it's just a little bigger than average instead of *massive*, I was sold on the idea of making him feel good—until he snatched me like that.

I should've known better than to doubt him. He put us both in a position where I was protected and he could enjoy my exploration of his body the same way he got to explore mine. As thoughtful as ever, he even made sure to muffle his own roar of release when he orgasmed.

Turns out Mal is a bit of a screamer, too.

As if drawn to me like a moth to a flame, my dazed demon follows my every move as I begin to head toward the bathroom.

"Shannon..." he says weakly.

I glance behind me.

"Already?" I ask. I can't help sounding so stunned. It has only been a couple of minutes or so since all of that come jetted out of him, and Mal's cock is already at half-mast. It's still solid, the reddish color almost purple as it continues to harden beneath my disbelieving stare.

Mal glances down. With his red demon skin, there's no way of knowing if he can blush the same way a human does, but I feel a rush of shame that doesn't belong to me.

Oh. I guess I'm getting better at picking up his emotions, too. Not with my nose, but with my gut.

He bats at his cock; it's already completely hard again. "It's often like this when you're around, my mate. I can not help it."

He might not be able to. But maybe I can.

If he looked at me like I hung the moon and the stars for just stroking him, how will he react when I do this?

Moving back toward him, I sink to my knees before Mal. His gasp of surprise is quickly replaced by his muttered groan as I close my mouth around the purple head of his erection.

He reaches down. Instead of gripping my head, using it so that he can fuck me in my mouth like too many old boyfriends have done, Mal runs his claws through my hair, caressing me while murmuring softly.

He's reverting to Sombran, but I know exactly what he's saying.

They're declarations of love, and they're all for me. About how I own his heart, how I'm the one and only female for him, and how he'll love me until the end of time no matter what I choose.

As I throw all of my effort into giving my virgin monster—because, surprise, he's managed to keep his V-card for *a thousand years*—his first blow job, I can't help but wonder:

Would it really be so bad to be mated to the monster?

CHAPTER 15
THE BEANERY

SHANNON

Later that night, when Mal grabs a pillow and begins to make himself a nest on my floor, I roll my eyes and pat the empty space next to me in my bed. Call me easy if you want, but after I both give and get oral sex from a guy, it seems kind of silly to refuse to sleep next to him.

My bed is a queen. It was the biggest I could fit into my bedroom, and I like how it gives me enough room to roll around at night. As Mal eases his weight onto the left side of the mattress, it seems more like a kiddie bed. He takes up more than half of the space, even scrunching his massive shoulders. Lying flat, his ankles hang over the edge of the bed. The points of his horns hit my headboard, gouging the wood.

It can't be comfortable. Cozier than the floor, sure,

but I try to scoot closer to the right side to give him a little more space.

Mal isn't having it. Rolling onto his side, his hand lands on my hip, tugging me into him. He's solid and firm, his chest warm against my back as he adjusts his body. Before I know it, he's the big spoon and I'm the little one, and we kind of actually fit.

What a difference a couple of days makes. On Saturday, I was just about shitting bricks, I was so scared. Now? I... I've never felt more safe and protected than I do with a monstrous demon at my back.

I wiggle when I sleep, too. Always have. Even if I fall asleep on my back, I inevitably toss and turn a couple of times so that the way I wake up is never the same as how I knock out. If Mal watched me like he said he did, he would've known that, but he doesn't complain as I move all night.

In fact, I kind of think he doesn't mind. Especially since, when I wake up, I find that my head is nestled against one huge pec. My arm is thrown across his waist; as big as he is, I don't even reach his other side. Hussy that I am, I've somehow wrapped both of my legs around his thigh like I was a dog humping him in my sleep or something. At least I'm wearing my pjs.

The blanket is gone. With the slight heat that continues to pour off of Mal, I must've tossed it sometime in the night. My monster is still wearing the shadow clothes he conjured just for me, but they definitely don't leave much to the imagination without the blanket covering him.

If you ever wondered if a demon got morning wood, I'm here to tell you that: yes. Yes, they do.

He has a tent forming that has me gaping at the sheer size of it. You'd think that I had gotten a little more comfortable with how huge his dick is after I had my hands—and mouth—all over it, but that's not the case. If anything, without lust clouding me, it seems even more unmanageable.

He wants to put that *inside* of me. That's his end game. Mal is being too much the gentleman demon to put the idea out there like that, but of all the things I am, naive isn't one of them. Mate *does* mean what I thought it meant. He wants to mount me and rut me and fuck me with that baseball bat between his legs.

It's one thing to fool around. I blame it on the whole essence-swapping and my long dry spell between partners. He treats my body like it's something precious, and he made me come harder than ever before. I mean, my legs were *shaking*. Then, despite his reassurance, I just had to return the favor.

That's it, though. That's as far as it can go. If I mate him, I'm stuck with him. He'll be another shadow, one I can never, ever get rid of.

Last night, I wondered if it would really be so bad. And, if I'm being honest, the answer is *not really* —but that doesn't change anything.

I like him. And maybe it's because he's not shy in

how much he adores me, but being around Mal is a constant esteem boost.

He can cook, too. It takes a few tries for him to get the hang of my stove, but once he understands that the blue flames on my gas burner do the same thing as a Sombra fire pit, he's a whiz at searing a steak or grilling some chicken. The boast he made that first night I met him, when he mentioned eating Earth plants, comes back to bite him in his tight ass when I introduce the concept of balanced meals to him.

He's generous in bed. He seems to get more pleasure out of making me come than he does when I go down on him.

Even after I finished blowing him the first time, letting him come in my fist again, he followed me into the bathroom to help me wash up. Somehow, that ended up with the both of us standing beneath the shower spray as he slowly stroked me to another orgasm. Then, holding me up against his big body, he used the fronts of his claws to massage my head as he leisurely washed my hair before cleaning the rest of my body for me.

It was so nice to shower with him that, the next morning, I invite him to join me in there again. And, sure, maybe it's a slippery slope; with the water sluicing down our bodies, soap slicking our flesh, I mean that literally. If he was any other guy, I would've said, *fuck it,* by then and, well, fucked him.

But I can't. Even if I could figure out how to make

us fit, it isn't worth a lifetime bond for a few moments of pleasure unless I'm absolutely sure that's what I want.

I don't want to toy with Mal. I never want to give him false hope, and if he's satisfied with what we have so far, then I'll give him everything I can.

And if I'm already beginning to lose my heart to him? Well… I'll figure that out before the gold moon deadline.

I have to.

THE SHOWER TAKES THE EDGE OFF OF MY NEED Thursday morning. With the rest of the week still scheduled as PTO so I can "recover" from my "illness", I introduce Mal to the wonderful world of binging TV while trying not to pay attention to just how… *right* it feels to be curled up against him on my couch.

I pointedly choose something that I enjoy, but that won't insult Mal. Supernatural was out, so was Grimm, and I settle on firing up one of my streaming services so that we can watch Bob's Burgers together.

Hey. He loves a good hamburger, and I love his laugh. It's a win-win.

We're almost at the end of the first season when my phone goes off later that afternoon.

That's weird. My phone doesn't usually ring

during the day. My parents don't bother me when they think I'm at work. Work won't call because I'm on PTO and Lisa believes that time is sacred. Even if a client needs to place an emergency order, she'll just route their calls and emails to one of my colleagues until I'm back.

Curious, I reach for my phone.

A beaming brunette stares up at me from the contact picture.

Yeah… I should've been expecting this call.

I met Tori McMahon through work. Her husband, Chris, has the cubicle next to mine, and I got a front row seat to all of their wedding planning last summer. Chris was *that guy* in the office, and his default was to put any and all calls on speaker.

Whatever the opposite of a bridezilla was, that was Tori. The third time she called up Chris, threatening to run off with the minister if she had to make one more decision on her own, I couldn't help but adore her.

Later, once I got to know her through work events —our Christmas party last year was when we became fast friends—I learned it was because Tori has a hard time making up her mind. She is *too* organized, if that's a thing, and she loses her head in all of the details.

Their wedding anniversary is coming up at the end of August. For some reason, they decided they should have a big party to celebrate, and while Chris booked the venue and hired the catering crew, Tori thought it might be easier to deal with the details this time.

Turns out it hasn't been, and that's where I've stepped in. Because I know them both pretty well but I'm also a neutral party, whenever Chris and Tori need a tie-breaker, they call me.

I can only imagine what this call is about. Probably whether or not Chris is allowed to do the Funky Chicken with his niblings after "the incident" at the wedding…

I tap the screen before holding my phone up to my ear. "Hey, Tori. What's up?"

"Shan, babe! How are ya?"

Hot and horny and thinking about asking a demon to touch me again. "I'm okay."

"Yeah? Chris told me you're out this week 'cause you're sick or something. I wanted to give you a couple of days to feel better, but I'm checking to see if we're still on for coffee?"

What? "Coffee?"

"Yeah. We're supposed to meet at The Beanery, remember? You're going to help me start the planning for my anniversary party, and I promised to buy you as many pastries and lattes as you wanted."

That's right. I did.

I pull my phone away from my ear, glancing at the time. It's three o'clock now, and we had made plans for five on Thursday evening. Normally, if I cut out of work a few minutes early, I could hit The Beanery by then. As a high school teacher, Tori's out by four, making it a perfect time to meet at our favorite café. I don't have work, and her school day is obviously over, and now she's double-checking our plans.

Ah, crap.

Mal's watching me curiously. In the background, Louise is giving her brother and sister a hard time, but instead of being glued to the cartoon like he has been for hours, his focus is solely on me.

I shrug, signaling that I'll explain when I'm off the phone, then tell Tori, "Uh, yeah. Sure. I'll be there."

She's my closest friend. These days, she's my *only* friend. And while PTO pays for me to miss work, I can't blow off Tori.

Even if I probably should.

———

MAL DIDN'T SAY ANYTHING WHEN I EXPLAINED THAT I made an evening coffee date Thursday night with Tori well before I knew anything about him. Even though he doesn't burn when we separate anymore, he insists on tagging along. Already running behind because I completely spaced until Tori called me, there's no time to argue with him.

Lately, I've been drinking the coffee that Mal brews for me in my old coffee pot. It gets the job done, but once I walk into The Beanery, there's no way I'm not getting a latte and a croissant to soak up the excess caffeine. I don't even wait for Tori to buy it for me.

Derek is as friendly as ever as he takes my order, and when he casually mentions he's missed me all week, I cling to my "I've been sick" excuse. I might as well. Tori is under the impression I've been out of work because of my "illness", too. Besides, it's not like I can tell anyone in my life why I'm really blowing off work and refusing to visit The Beanery while Mal is still with me.

Tori isn't here yet. My friend is always exactly on time, and it's a few minutes before five. At this hour, The Beanery is fairly empty, and I snag us a table in the far corner where Mal can comfortably hide in the shadows beneath it.

I'd warned him to be quiet. I knew he wouldn't let anyone see him, but his promise to keep his mouth shut lasts only as long as takes for me to settle into my seat after making sure he's completely hidden.

"Can't we invite your female friend back to your home?" murmurs Mal. "I'll hide so she can't see me."

"Shh. It's fine. We won't be here long."

That's… probably not true. Knowing Tori, we'll most likely be here until the café closes and the closing barista kicks out us.

Speaking of the barista—

Mal huffs. "I don't think we should stay. I don't like that male."

Ah, jeez. I thought Mal didn't really pay Derek any attention when we were in The Beanery on Sunday, but I was careful not to come back with the demon just in case. He never mentioned how Derek asked me out to dinner, and I guess I'd just about managed to convince myself that he didn't understand that Derek had been making a move on me.

"Don't," I say under my breath. "Drop it, okay?"

"Hmm?"

He can't possibly think I buy that confused murmur. "Come on, Mal. You know what I mean."

"Do I?"

Oh. He wants to do this the hard way? Fine.

"Derek's just a friend," I tell him, keeping my voice low in case anybody nearby wonders why I'm seemingly talking to myself. I've already had the guy nursing his coffee in one corner giving me sly looks so I'm not sure I'm doing that great of a job. "He makes a good latte and he's nice, so stop it."

"Nice?" echoes Mal. "He lusts after my mate."

You've gotta be kidding me. Is Mal *pouting?*

I glance around The Beanery again. That guy is looking at me, and so is Derek.

Great.

"Whoops," I announce loudly as I "accidentally" knock my stack of napkins fluttering to the floor beneath my table.

Ducking beneath it, I should be able to have a

quick, whispered conversation without drawing too much attention. At least, I *hope* I can.

"He doesn't lust after me."

"He does," repeats Mal. "It's in his scent. When he looks at you, it's undeniable."

"What do you mean, his scent? You can't *smell* that… can you?"

"Of course I can, my mate."

Wait… "Can you smell *me*?"

"A Sombra demon's nose is very powerful. When it comes to you, I can scent all your moods. Your anger burns like fire, and your laughter is sweet like syrup, and your lust…" Mal's tone goes impossibly low. "It's *delicious*."

"Keep your voice down," I whisper harshly. It's unnecessary since Mal's already so quiet, it's doubtful anyone can hear him, but fuck if I'm not super embarrassed right now. All those times I looked at him and wondered what it would be like to touch him, or to let him touch me, before we became intimate… and he *knew*?

"Don't be ashamed. Your body responding to me is natural. After all, you are my mate."

"I'm not ashamed!" I snap back.

"Shannon?"

Clunk.

"Damn it!"

At the sound of my name, I had jerked my head

up so quickly, I whacked it against the table. Because I wasn't already embarrassed, now I'm in pain, too.

Mal doesn't say anything now that he knows we have company, but he does reach out with the edge of his shadow. I slap at him, muttering a curse under my breath, then slowly climb out from beneath the café table.

Tori is standing in front of it, her dark brown hair piled high in a ponytail, an oversized white binder tucked beneath her arm.

She's watching me with a bemused expression. "You okay, Shan?"

I'm not seeing stars, but it's pretty close. I poke the part of my head that's throbbing the most. Crap. I've already got a lump.

"Yeah," I say, rubbing the lump for good measure. I'd kill for an Advil, but since I was the idiot who jumped when I heard my name, I'll just have to deal for now. "Yeah, I'm okay."

"You sure? 'Cause I know you've been feeling like crap, but if you're talking to your shoes, maybe you should be in bed."

Right. With Mal melted into the shadows beneath the table, it must've looked like I was having a very heated discussion with my sneakers.

I shake my head. "I'm alright. Just annoyed I, uh, dropped all my napkins."

"Good. Because we have a lot of decisions to

make." She shows me the binder, waving it at me as she says in a sing-song voice, "I have print-outs."

That's such a Tori thing to do. Organized to a fault, she must have options for every element of her upcoming anniversary party. She'll weigh the pros and cons before making any decisions, and she'll ask me my opinion on each one.

That binder is at least three inches thick. I was right. We're definitely going to be here for a while.

"Crank that bad boy open," I tell her. "Let's get started."

CHAPTER 16

THE PROMISE OF FRIDAY

SHANNON

I pat the side of the table opposite of me, hoping like heck that Tori doesn't accidentally bump into Mal when she sinks down in her seat. When I feel him brush against me, wrapping his shadows around my legs like the most faithful puppy, I know I was worrying about nothing.

Chains, I remember. If anyone else finds out Mal is on our plane, he'll end up in chains.

As Tori starts flipping through the first section—color schemes—I put my elbow on the table, cupping my chin in my hand. For the first time since I've met the demon, it hits me that I have a pretty easy out if I wanted to take it. All I'd have to do is make it so that someone besides me saw Mal. Then, *poof*, that green-eyed demon would appear and I could wash my hands of the whole thing.

The second that occurs to me, I quickly banish the thought. Maybe on Saturday night when I was freaking out, I might've been able to do that. Now? I'm not saying that I'm ready to spend the rest of my life with a shadow monster who will undoubtedly outlive me, but it would be fucking *cruel* to sentence him to chains and a dungeon just so my life can go back to the way it was.

Whatever happens, happens, but it's not going to be because I was too much of a chicken to decide whether or not I could actually be a demon's mate.

For the next half an hour, I go cross-eyed at all the print-outs she shows me. Selecting a color scheme went fairly quickly, as did the type of cake she wanted to order, but when we got to the party dress, I decided it was time for a quick break from the binder.

I'd already eaten half of my croissant, subtly dropping the other half to Mal's waiting grasp, and I was thinking about grabbing another when Tori shoves the binder away from her, a devilish gleam in her pretty green eyes.

I don't like it.

"What?"

"Nothing. I was just thinking it's a good idea for you to go over there and order us a couple of pastries. I owe you."

Nope. Still don't like it.

"Why?"

"Why not?" As I keep quiet, waiting for Tori to expound on that, she flips her ponytail behind her. "So, I was also thinking… we're feminists, right? Who says you can't take a chance and go for the man you want?"

"I'm good in the man department right now," I say hurriedly.

Tori raises her eyebrows. "Oh? So you have a date for the party and forgot to mention it to me, your bestest best friend?"

"No, but—"

"Why don't you ask Derek?"

Oh, *hell*.

"Tori. I don't—"

She's determined. That's Tori, all right. "Go on, Shan. See if Derek's free to come with you to the party."

"I promise. I'm okay." Beneath the table, the space where Mal is folded up in shadow form has suddenly grown uncomfortably warm. Even if I wanted to pretend he didn't understand what my friend meant, his reaction makes that impossible. I have to change the subject. Tapping at the picture of a sleeveless pink dress, I say, "Now, what do you think about this one?"

Tori waves her hand. "The dress can wait, babe. Look. There's no customers and, let me tell you, Derek's been watching you whenever he gets the chance ever since I got here. Go on. Make your move."

If he's watching me, it's probably because he's trying to figure out when exactly I lost my damn mind. Between bursting into the shop after I first summoned Mal, to begging him to give me Kennedy's information, then kind of, sort of blowing off *his* offer of a date?

Plus the way I was talking to myself since he can't see Mal?

Yeah… that ship has sailed, and not only because my feelings for him have inexplicably changed.

"I don't think that's a good idea, Tor."

"Why not?"

Crap. How could I have forgotten just how pushy Tori can be?

"I don't know. But let's drop it."

I know her well enough to tell that she's not going to. Probably because she honestly believes she's helping me, and also because she's so stinking happy with Chris, she wants everyone around her to be hooked up so they can be happy, too. She couldn't believe that I hadn't even had a one-night stand in the last three years, let alone a date, and all because I chose to be single for a while.

I could only imagine her reaction when she discovers I have a new FWB; he just happens to have horns, is immortal, and came from a demon plane. If Mal makes me happy, Tori won't give a shit about any of that, and next thing I know she'll have a binder that details whatever kind of marriage-type ceremony they have in Sombra.

Oh, yeah. Gotta change the subject and make it stick.

Luckily, my phone picks the perfect moment to vibrate.

Yes.

"Hold that thought, Tori." I grab my phone, prepared for another marketing text from one of those companies I keep forgetting to unsubscribe from.

But it isn't.

A rush of excitement slams into me when I see that the notification is actually an email from—

Oh my god.

Amy.

I quickly click it, expanding it so that I can read past the first couple of lines.

Hi Shannon,

Sorry about the late reply. I got your message a few days ago, but I've been figuring out how exactly to answer it. Honestly, I almost junked it, thinking it couldn't be true. No one knows about Sombra... at least, they're not supposed to. But since you seem to know even more than that, maybe it's a good idea that we meet, just like you suggested.

How about tomorrow afternoon? I'm off of work at four and we can meet you then.

I pause.

We? Who the heck is *we*?

Returning to the screen, I see that she ends the email with an address and her phone number, plus a note that invites me to call her if I want to. She assures me that it's safe, and that she hopes that I bring my shadow with me.

Suddenly, I understand what *we* means. Even if that photo is nearly two decades old, she must still have *hers*.

That means there's another Sombra demon on Earth.

That seals it for me. Most of her message doesn't come out and *say* that, and maybe I'm too hopeful for a lead that I'm reading too much into it, but I'm suddenly very eager for it to be Friday.

I FEEL BAD, BUT AFTER I TAPPED OUT A REPLY TO Amy's message that I'd love to meet up with them, I totally made up a bogus excuse to give to Tori. Something about how I was starting to feel a little queasy again, and that I'll be more than happy to reschedule with her to finish up with the rest of her party planning.

Remembering what Mal said, I told her we could

meet at my place some time next week if she wanted, and in her good-natured way, Tori agreed, "Long as you Lysol the shit out of your place, babe."

As soon as we were out on the street outside of The Beanery, I could tell that Mal wanted to say something. Since I wasn't in the mood to rehash our argument over Derek from before, I cut him off quickly, telling him all about Amy's email.

Since I had pointed out the shadow in Amy's photo for him to confirm that it was another demon from his world, I couldn't keep the message I sent to her from Mal. It didn't seem right. Even as we spent the last few days learning each others' bodies, I never once gave him the impression that I'd given up on finding him a way back to Sombra. At this point, I figured I was stuck with him until the gold moon rose —whenever *that* is, and I still don't know since Mal refuses to tell me—but it wouldn't hurt to meet with another human woman who knows about Sombra demons.

When I look it up, the address Amy sent me is a three-hour drive out from Jericho. I guess it could've been worse. What if she had moved to Timbuktu in the time since the spellbook was local enough to fall into Kennedy's hands? Instead of a day trip with Mal, I could've been trying to figure out how I could sneak my shadow monster onto a cross-Atlantic flight.

It's a house, too. A little more internet sleuthing and I'm surprised to discover that the deed belongs to

Susanna M. Benoit, the previous owner of my spell-book. Looks like it passed on to Amy after her aunt was legally declared dead a few years ago.

From what I can tell, everything seems like it's on the up and up. If not, at least I'm not going alone. I have no doubt that Mal would do anything he had to to keep me safe, even if it comes to facing off against another Sombra demon.

And I believe that for, oh, about ten seconds after Amy opens the door to her ranch-style house, inviting both me and my shadow into her home, and I get my first look at her mate.

This is obviously a home treated for a shadow monster. The ceilings are high, the windows treated so that little light gets in, and no nosy nearby neighbors could get a peek of the towering monster who appears as soon as Amy closes the door.

Mal is huge. He's seven feet tall with muscles as big as freaking basketballs in his demon form. The shadow monster who winks into existence is at least six inches taller than Mal, though his build is more lean. His horns arc around his head, almost like a crown, and his hair is only as long as his pointed chin.

Now, I knew that all Sombra demons didn't have yellow eyes like Mal. After all, Glaine's were green. And Amy's mate?

His are a vibrant red.

When he first appears, he's the inky black shadow monster that hovers an inch or two off of the floor.

After a few seconds when I take him in, he solidifies; he has the same dark red skin as Mal, though it's closer to the color of rust. On his chest, he's marked with runes similar to the ones that appeared in gold on Mal's shadowy arms when he first arrived in the human world. They're not gold, but silver, and I get the idea that I'm looking at what the Sombra demons consider body art.

Thankfully, he also wears shadow coverings that leave his cock covered if his chest bare.

Amy is probably a couple of inches taller than me, though she appears tiny when she moves to stand next to her mate. He drops his solid hand on her shoulder, the touch overly possessive. When he shifts again to his shadow form, he keeps his hand firmly there.

Seeing the other shadow monster is almost enough to knock out the surprise I felt when I first met Amy at the door. I had called when I was about a half an hour out to let her know that we were still coming, and I introduced myself as Shannon Crewes at the door. She confirmed she was Amy, then let us in.

I mean, she looks like the profile picture I found online.

Like, *exactly*.

Same face. Same hair, though the style is shorter than it was. She's wearing a light blue sundress that brings out her eyes and the few blonde streaks in her mahogany-colored hair.

No wrinkles, I notice. No obvious sign that she had any work done, either. If I didn't know better, I'd think she was barely my age—but *how*?

Amy smiles warmly at me. I realize that I've started to stare at her and I quickly clear my throat. Waving my hand, a signal I agreed upon with Mal during the car ride, he materializes at my side. We decided that he would stay out of sight until she proved that she, too, had a Sombra demon for a mate. If Amy already knew about the shadow-based demon race, it should be okay for her to see Mal, and glancing back at her towering mate, no doubt that that cat has long been out of the bag.

"This is Mal," I say, making introductions.

"Malphas," grunts Amy's mate. After squeezing her shoulder, he moves forward, clasping Mal on his.

I look up at him. His expression has me going a little worried there. Why… why does Mal look super uncomfortable all of a sudden?

"You okay, big guy? You know each other or something?"

He nods, though he doesn't look away from the red-eyed demon as he goes back to Amy. And that's saying something because Mal rarely takes his eyes off of me. "Yes. I… yes."

Amy's eyes shoot to her mate. "Nox. Is this okay?"

I know exactly what she's asking. I'm wondering the same thing, too. I didn't want to assume that all Sombra demons knew each other—Mal already said their plane was too big for that—but this is a little weird. What if they were enemies back in their world? Amy's mate—Nox—greeted Mal without any aggression, but does that really mean anything?

Nox nods. Immediately, Amy relaxes. "Thank you, baby."

Well, if I had any doubt that these two were happily mated, I don't have them anymore. I guess, somewhere in the back of my head, I'd wondered if her monster had forced her into mating him. Not that I ever expected Mal would do that to me—I'm absolutely sure he would *never*—but he's one demon out of thousands. They can't all be gentleman demons like mine.

And this guy? Something tells me that he's no gentleman.

"Well," Amy says, brighter than before. "I'm Amy. This is my mate, Nox. Wow. I… I can't believe this. For almost fifteen years, I thought I was the only one who Fate gave one of these amazing males to. I'm so glad to meet you guys."

Fifteen… fifteen *years*?

Welp. Either I'm missing something, or maybe I was wrong for assuming that they had a mutual bonding thing going on…

After reaching down, squeezing Nox's hand—it's solid again—Amy gestures to me. "I'm sure you have a thousand questions. You mentioned some in your email, and I thought it would be easier if I answered them in person. Thank you so much for making the drive. Nox… he doesn't like cars."

"If you've been dragged beneath one like I have, you wouldn't either," he grumbles.

Oh. Okay, then.

Amy lifts her hand, rubbing his arm. He's back to his shadowy form. "Anyway, I was thinking we can go in the den and talk. Maybe leave the males to reminisce about Sombra. What do you think?"

Do I really want to be separated from Mal? The fact that my initial instinct is *no* makes me forge ahead with Amy's suggestion.

"Sure. Lead the way."

CHAPTER 17
AMY & NOX

SHANNON

The den is only down the hall and a room away from the entrance to Amy's home. There's a leather couch against the far wall, and as she waves at me to take a seat, I notice that it's covered in a countless amount of deep slices.

"Sorry about that. Sometimes Nox can't control his claws, and it's better me than the couch. I can always replace a couch, right? If it bothers you, I can grab a blanket to lay down."

"No. I'm fine." Curious as heck, but fine. Why doesn't her mate do the trick with his claws that Mal does? Is it because he doesn't know to, or does it have something to do with how he keeps switching forms? Good questions, but not the most pressing one on my mind.

"Okay. I'm sorry if this is rude as hell, but I can't help it. How old are you? Because you just said you've been with Nox for fifteen years and—"

"Actually," she cuts in, her lips twitching slightly in a slight smile, "I've known Nox for more than thirty years. We only finalized our bonding fifteen years ago."

See? That's exactly what's bothering me.

"*How?*"

She was smiling, but it wavers just enough to have me wondering if I made a big boo boo there asking. I get the feeling that there's definitely something I'm missing now.

"Um. Shannon. How old do you think I actually am?"

I look her over. I'm twenty-nine, so maybe she's… "Twenty-six?"

"I'm forty-one."

I blink. "Wow. You look good for forty-one. You gotta give me some skincare tips, girl."

Amy chuckles softly. "You already have everything you need. If you mate with Malphas, you'll stop aging, too."

"*What?*"

Her chuckle dies out quickly as she suddenly frowns at the way my voice went high-pitched like that. "Didn't he tell you?"

Tell me that monster jizz is better than Oil of Olay? "Uh. No. No, he did not."

"But you know he's basically immortal, right?"

That I did. When I first found out that Mal waited more than a thousand years for me, I thought he was being dramatic. Nope. There are no diseases in Sombra, no old age, either. They stop aging when they hit their peak form, forever strong and powerful. Unless their duke orders their execution, they will never die. Even in my world, Mal is untouchable.

How do you kill a demon who can go as insubstantial as shadow in the blink of an eye?

Me, on the other hand... I figured I had another fifty, sixty years. I started this thing with my monster —whatever it is—knowing that he would outlive me.

Does the revelation that monster dick comes with a side of immortality make the prospect of mating Mal a little more attractive? I... I don't know. If I lived forever and still aged, that would be a hard no. But to be eternally twenty-nine?

Not gonna lie, there's something tempting about never hitting thirty.

"You see," Amy continues, "I met Nox when I was nine. I thought he was the bogeyman, then an imaginary friend, before he disappeared when I was twelve. He found me again when I actually was twenty-six so, technically, you're right, too. As soon as I bonded with Nox, making him mine, I stopped aging. You will, too."

"Me? Oh, no. I... I'm not trying to mate him." Why does that sound like a lie to me even as I say it? I shake my head. "I mentioned it in my email. When I told you that I found you through the spellbook? I was hoping you could give me some idea how to reverse the spell and send him home."

At least, when I first emailed Amy, I'd been hoping that. Now, I'm really more interested in finding out why a human woman would give up their life as they knew it to bond with a Sombra demon.

Oh, and how that spellbook fell into my hands in the first place.

At the mention of the book, Amy's whole expression changes.

"The *Grimoire du Sombra*… My aunt loved that stupid thing. I was just a kid, and when she disappeared, I took it from her house. This house, actually. I came with my mom and I stole it. I mean, I was a little girl. Barely nine. I saw her handwriting, and I couldn't help but think that that page… that one page… could tell me where she went. Only, when a shadow appeared, it wasn't Aunt Su who came through. It was Nox. Aunt Su was gone, but at least I had my shadow man."

I want to ask her about her Aunt Su. That must be Susanna M. Benoit, but she sounds so sad when she mentions her, it's obvious that, all these years later, Susanna is still gone.

Legally dead, I remember. No wonder she's sad.

Even though I told her in my message, I say, "I bought the book on a whim. A place called Turn the

Page in Jericho, New York. I never thought the spell would work, but jokes on me, I guess, because I've had a demon roomie"—a demon lover—"for almost a week now. And, okay, I'll admit we've gotten close. But I've gone through that book a bunch of times now and I can't figure out how to break this bond between us and send him home where he belongs."

Amy's brow wrinkles. I don't think she was expecting me to say that. "Why would you? You're his fated mate. In Sombra, that means he's yours. Why wouldn't you take him as your mate? Here... Sombra... he belongs with you, Shannon."

Is it nuts that I believe that, too?

"Okay," she says, "let me try to help. When it comes to you and Malphas, what's holding you back?"

I open my mouth. Think about how to answer that question. Close it.

What *is* holding me back?

Before, I might've used the age gap—and the fact that I'll be dead in what amounts to a blink of the eye to Mal—as a cop-out. Or how I'll never be able to introduce him as my lover to anyone besides Amy and Nox. I can't bring Mal to Chris and Tori's party, and I'll have to take a ventriloquist class or two so that I can talk to his faded shadow form without people wanting to call out the little men in white coats on me.

All valid reasons. But when I think about how precious Mal makes me feel, and the promises he makes in Sombran when he thinks I've already fallen asleep in his arms… I keep on wondering, what if?

Amy can tell.

She rests her hand on my knee, and when I glance at her, I can see the weight of those forty-one years in her eyes.

"I can't help you decide whether or not Malphas is the one for you. I always knew that my fate was tied to Nox, and when he came for me, mating him was never in doubt. I mean, we had our own problems"—Amy gets a faraway look as she says that, and I can only imagine what she's remembering—"but I always knew he was it for me once I knew he still existed. But if you *do* decide to take Malphas as your mate, I've got a trick or two that might help."

My ears perk up. "I'm listening…"

MALPHAS

The last time I saw Nox, he was in chains.

That was a couple of decades ago. I don't know how many. Though he was from my clan, when he disappeared from Nuit only to return with his hands bound in a length of golden chain, I knew that he had offended Duke Haures. Those who do only do so once. I expected he'd be dragged to the dungeons of Mavro, the capital of Sombra, never to be heard from again.

Now I know why.

Sombra itself is a vast plane. There are more clans than I can count. Odds were that I would've never known the Sombra demon who was mated to the human Amy. And, yet, I do. From his glowing red eyes to his fierce expression, I recognize the most well-known hunter of my clan.

He knows me, too. Clapping me on the shoulder, a greeting more fit to the mortal world than our stoic demon realm, Nox meets me like an old friend.

He no longer is in chains. Inside of Amy's home, he moves freely, switching between his demon and shadow forms sometimes in between footfalls. I've heard of that happening before. When a demon's essence is too weak to stay in one shape, switching becomes out of our control.

It's not Duke Haures's harshest punishment. That would be an execution, reserved for only the worst criminals in Sombra. A never-ending imprisonment in the dungeons is next, but only for those he wants to see squirm.

And then there are the golden chains. Forged from iron that's been charmed during the night of the gold moon, it's the closest we can get to being stripped of our power and our essence. The chains weaken a Sombran until death would be preferable, and for a mated male, they interfere with the bond we share with our females. It's why Glaine threatened me with chains when he confronted me on the duke's orders. A Sombra demon who doesn't claim their mate before the next gold moon risks going fully demonic—a fate that Duke Haures's regime refuses to allow so long as he is in charge.

He's been the ruler of Sombra for nearly two thousand years now. The chains are a very credible threat.

They work. Like a mate's promise, they're virtually unbreakable, too—but here's Nox, and though his wrists are inky black even when he's in his red-skinned demon form, he's chain-free.

I want to ask, but with my mate standing within reach of Nox's claws, my only aim was in keeping her safe and protected from the scowling demon.

As a hunter, Nox had a reputation for being quick and brutal when it came to his kills. He had no mercy, and often looked down on me for being the clan artist. I never minded. We each have our calling, and I could never take a life the way he could, even if it meant I went without meat at times.

That was why the clan wasn't so surprised when he ended up in chains. Hunters are closer to their demon side, and are often the ones who choose to leave clan life behind, disappearing into the far-reaching shadows of Sombra. Eventually, they become a threat to the way the duke rules over our plane.

I never knew what Nox did to earn his punishment. While mingling with humans and letting them learn about Sombra is the duke's first law, it's only the first of many.

And, yet, here he is. Living in the mortal realm, his chest marked with Sombran runes to spell out the name of his mate: *Amelia*. The silver gleams as brightly as it must have the day he carved her name in his chest, though the scars around the edge of the mark are old. He's been mated for long enough that the tattoo is now a part of him.

Still, when he gazes upon his Amy, there's a besotted expression only rivaled by the possessive gleam in his red eyes.

I probably look upon my Shannon the same way.

After introductions are made, the females disappear into another room. While my immediate reaction is to follow Shannon, it's actually Nox who grips me by my shoulder, holding me back.

"Let them talk," he grunts. "The females want privacy. As their mates, we will give it to them."

"Play nice, big guy," Shannon calls out to me, blue eyes alive with humor. "Don't ram your horns or anything, okay?"

Nox frowns. "Why would we do that? If a horn breaks, it takes centuries to regrow it. No male would do that."

Shannon winks. "Just making sure," she says, then disappears around a corner.

Nox turns to me. "Your mate is a strange creature."

"She is," I agree, my chest puffing with pride. She's my Shannon, and I'm grateful the gods and Fate both chose her for me. "There's none better. And you? What of your mate?"

"She is my world. I'm nothing without her."

I glance down at the burn marks on his wrists. "You were in chains."

He gives a sharp nod. "I was."

"Because of her?"

Nox pulls back his lips, showing off his fangs. "I wore the chains *for* my mate. I knew not to touch her. I knew to keep my distance. I knew that, if she saw me, I would have to mate her or face the duke. When I failed, I *chose* my punishment."

There were rumors among the clan that Nox went to Duke Haures's dungeon too willingly. That, as a powerful hunter, he was a fair match to Glaine and the other guards that the duke sent after him. None of us knew he'd been to the human world, only that he'd broken a Sombran law. He could've avoided the dungeons and the chains, living in the wild shadows if he wanted to.

But he didn't. He allowed Glaine and Sammael to capture him. The last time I saw Nox was when he marched out of Nuit with his horns high and his wrists clamped in golden chains.

Nox slants a look my way. In the quiet following his admission, he calms enough to lower his voice so that we don't disturb the females.

"When I met my Amy, she was a child. Not even a *decade*, Malphas."

My mouth falls open. I tried to explain to Shannon in the aftermath of Glaine finding me that Sombra demons age differently than humans. With such an extended lifespan, we grow until we reach our full maturity—when we're about three centuries old—and then we stay at our physical peak. I've seen so many more years than my mate, but we're at the same level of maturity. We're both adults and ready to be true mates.

A demon is a child until their first century. The idea of looking at a girl demon of that age makes me shudder in revulsion. And Nox discovered his mate when she was even younger?

"I'm so sorry, Nox."

"Don't be," he says sharply. "The chains kept me contained until my mate was mature enough for a male. And when the time was right... when she needed me most... I broke the chains so I could get to her."

Ah. Now I understand why his wrists look the way they do, and the reason behind his inability to hold forms. To feed the cursed chains enough to break, he would've had to sacrifice almost more essence than he could spare.

And he did it for his mate.

Just like I would do anything for my Shannon.

Nox knows. Whether he's remembering his time

with his mate, or he can see how much I care for mine written in every harsh line of my face, my former clansman knows exactly what I'm thinking now.

Nox claps me on the shoulder again. Any posturing between two Sombra demons falls away as he realizes that I'm exactly what he once was: a lovesick male desperate to please his fated female.

"Human mates are nothing like we were led to expect," he grates out, "but they're worth whatever it takes to claim them."

Taking his hand back, he raises both of his arms, showing off his ruined wrists. "Anything."

I believe him.

CHAPTER 18
MAL'S GIFT

SHANNON

During the long drive back to Jericho, I can't stop thinking about some of the things Amy said to me.

The whole idea that Mal can share his immortality with me is huge. Let's put that right out there. I thought I'd have maybe another fifty, sixty years, tops, and it's nuts to think that I could keep on existing as I am all because some faceless force known as Fate decided I would be the perfect mate to Malphas of Sombra.

I'm just Shannon. I'm an account manager, even though I always wanted to be a botanist; my fixation with flowers has been a part of me for as long as I can remember, but my parents pushed me into a business degree when I went to college. What did I do to deserve a sexy demon for a mate who could offer me forever—and actually *mean* it?

And traveling… once… *if…* I agree to take Mal as my mate, it isn't only the rest of the human world I can explore. Claiming a Sombra mate is like instant citizenship to their world. I could visit Sombra, or even one of the neighboring planes as long as Mal came with me.

It's definitely something to think about.

Good thing I have time. Not much, since I'm racing the freaking moon, but it's not like I have to decide tonight.

Mal's quiet, too. When I prod him to open up about the other demon, he confirms how he knows Amy's mate. Turns out they're from the same clan. What are the odds? It must have something to do with Amy's aunt's spellbook. As a kid, Amy did the same thing I did. She read the spell and, though she didn't actually mate Nox until much later, she manifested him the same way I brought Mal to me.

I asked her how she got around the deadline. I had to. She made it fifteen years before they mated, but as big a help as Amy was, she can't give me advice about the deadline because they *didn't* get around it; at least, Nox didn't. He was chained in the duke's dungeons the fifteen years they were separated until Nox finally found his way back to her.

I've never met this duke, but, holy shit, I already hate the guy.

Following Amy and Nox's path is out. Even if I never see Mal again, I can't let him go in chains. He doesn't deserve it. He deserves a mate that recognizes what a great male he is, and who will be the perfect mate for him.

I just… I don't know if that's me. And since he swears that a Sombra demon only ever gets one, that's a pretty big problem right there.

I like him. We're amazing together in bed. After a conversation with Amy that started out awkward and ended with the two of us giggling like schoolgirls, she let me in on the secret of how to make me and Mal *work* if I decide to go all the way with him.

Only one problem. If I do? There is no take-backs. We're bound for life, and now I have to grapple with what *that* means.

But I have time. I keep reminding myself that as we make our way back to Jericho and I pull into the parking spot provided by my apartment complex. Since it's late, the sun already set, Mal is in the more solid version of his shadow form. Still inky black, but after he slips through the open window, he meets me on the other side of my door.

He pops it open for me, my demon every inch the perfect gentleman.

I bump my shoulder against his elbow. It's about as high as I can reach. "Come on, Mal. I'm beat. Let's go to bed."

With a nod, he guides me to the back entrance of

the apartment building. It's only as he nearly disappears as he fades that I realize that, for the first time since I've known him, he didn't say, "As you wish," when I gave him an opening to.

Huh.

Shaking my head, I lead us to the elevator that'll bring us right to the fourth floor.

As I stick my key into the lock on my door, I hear another one open. Whirling around, I make sure that Mal has melted into the shadows at the end of the hall, then glance in time to see Mrs. Winslow stepping out of her apartment.

Ugh. Too slow. If I was quicker, I could've dodged her by disappearing inside of mine. Or, failing that, I could've asked Mal to hide me in the shadows with him again.

But I didn't, and now I have to play nice with Mrs. Winslow.

She's carrying a huge brown box in her arms. "Shannon. There you are."

"Evening, Mrs. Winslow." There's still a chance I can cut off this conversation. I turn my key quickly, trying to get my door open before I have to deal with my neighbor.

"I've been waiting for you to come home. Kind of late, isn't it?"

Kind of nosy, aren't you?

I smile, using my shoulder to shove my door in, then wait for a few seconds. The shadows shift, a rush of warmth slipping past me as Mal goes inside first. Now it's my turn. I nod. "Good night, Mrs. Winslow."

"Don't you want your package?"

My what?

She chuckles when she sees my blank expression. Hefting the oversized box in her arms, she tells me, "This has been outside of your door for a couple of hours. When you didn't answer, I brought it in for safekeeping. It's awfully heavy, Shannon, dear."

What the heck is wrong with me? That's my box, I guess, and I'm standing here while she struggles under its weight.

"Sorry." I scurry over to her, holding out my arms to take it. As she tilts it into my hold, I let out an *oof*. She wasn't wrong. This is freaking *heavy*. "Thanks."

"Don't mention it. Us neighbors have to look out for each other." With a jerk of her pointed chin at the box, she asks, "So, what did you order? Big box like that… it has me curious."

Of course it does. Resisting the urge to roll my eyes, I look down at the label. I see that it's addressed to Shannon Crewes—so, yup, definitely mine—but, for the life of me, I can't imagine what this could be. I have a habit of impulse buying things online when I'm bored, or when I remember I need something and I can actually wait for it to be delivered. But with everything going on since Mal appeared in my life, I can honestly say I haven't been bored at all…

Oh. Wait. I *do* know what this is. The return address only confirms it.

The smile that tugs on my lips is genuine. "Painting supplies. I bought some painting supplies. For art."

From the way her forehead wrinkles like that, I bet that she'd spent the whole night wondering only to be disappointed by the reveal. She was probably hoping it was a giant box of dildos or something equally as personal.

"Oh. That's nice. I didn't know you painted."

"I don't." My grin widens at how her expression is even more confused. "Thanks for getting my package for me, Mrs. Winslow. Good night!"

With a bounce in my step despite how awkward it is to hold the oversized box, I leave my neighbor in the hall. The door to my apartment is still open, and I let myself in, using my heel to kick it shut.

The second I do, Mal appears in front of me. I have no doubt in my mind that he lingered near the doorway, close in case I needed him.

"I shall carry this for you," he rumbles, easing the box out of my hold.

"Might as well," I say, "since it's yours."

"Mine?"

"Yup."

It's all coming back to me now. I bought it the other night. Mal rarely fell asleep before I did. He wasn't kidding when he said that Sombrans didn't need to rest as much as humans did, and he's usually up before me, too. That night, though, I must've really worn him out because he was out first.

I took advantage of it. Grabbing my phone, I placed an order for everything I thought he could use. So sure he'd wake up and catch me, I didn't have much time for research, so I kind of got a little bit of everything.

I didn't do it for any other reason than I wanted to surprise him. If our time together came to an end, then it could be a nice thing for him to remember me by. He had mentioned how he preferred to paint, but all of his supplies came from Soleil, a neighboring world.

So I bought him some Earth paints, a couple of brushes, and a bunch of canvases.

My shipping confirmation said to expect the box on Monday. I guess the delivery service was quicker than promised because it arrived today. I almost thought about making him wait until the morning at least, but he's been so... so *quiet* since we left Amy's.

"Open it now," I prod. "I want to make sure you like it."

Mal bends low, nuzzling the top of my head with his chin. "If it's from my Shannon, I'll adore it regardless."

I'm not so bushed that I don't roll my eyes at him. "Please?"

"As you wish," murmurs Mal as my heart skips a

beat.

Oh, yeah. There's my monster.

I cling to his side, watching as he uses a pointed claw to tear open the tape. I'm just about bouncing in place as he slowly opens each flap before reaching inside.

"Shannon…" The way he breathes out my name in awe like that makes me think I hit a home run with my gift. "You got this for me?"

"Sure did, big guy. I've seen the kind of magic you can work with chalk. I can't wait to see what you can do with paint."

Using the same claw that opened the box, Mal presses it gently to the underside of my chin, tilting my head back. He's gotten so much better at looking down at me, reading my expression before he rushes ahead to take my mouth in one of his hot and heavy kisses.

Tonight, his kiss is soft. Sweet. I can feel all the emotion thrumming through him almost as much as the need, and he kisses me to make sure that I do.

"Thank you," he rumbles as he pulls away from me. His breath warms my face as he sighs. "Fate couldn't have chosen a better mate for me than you, my Shannon."

I pat Mal's chest. Now that I have his essence, his heat soothes me the same way a soak in a hot tub does. It no longer stings or burns me, another sign that we're closer and closer to the point of no return.

Fate couldn't have chosen a better mate for me than you...

I freaking wish that was true—and I worry that it isn't.

I FALL ASLEEP WRAPPED UP IN MAL'S ARMS. ALL THOSE hours on the road took a bigger toll on me than I expected, and as soon as he looks at each color of paint I picked out for him, I tell him that I'm heading to bed.

After changing into my pjs and brushing my teeth, I curl up on my mattress, ready to pass out for the night. I told him I was perfectly fine with him playing with his new supplies, but he followed behind me, holding me close until I drifted off to sleep.

When I wake up the next morning, he's still there with me. He's not asleep, his golden eyes watching me as he strokes my hair lightly with his hand, but I'm surprised that he's not already up and about. Ever since I took his essence, we no longer have to stay up each other's butts; one of the consequences that didn't piss me off when I first discovered what letting him give me his essence actually meant. I know he'll never leave the apartment without me, but he's had free rein for a few days now.

"Morning," I murmur to Mal. "You just get up?"

He shakes his head, long black hair swaying with the motion. No matter how long he sleeps—a couple of hours, or the entire night beside me—his silky hair always looks like he's fresh from the salon. I'd hate him if I didn't like him so damn much.

"I've been awake for a while," he says, "but I could sense you were rousing soon, so I came back to bed. After all, the best part of waking up—"

"Is Folger's in your cup?" I tease. It was something my mom always said to me as she brewed coffee in the morning. I know that Mal won't get the reference, but I couldn't help myself.

In the beginning, Mal would frown when I made comments like that. Lately, he just smiles warmly in a way that says: Yes, my mate is different, but she's *my* mate and I wouldn't have her any other way.

"No," he corrects earnestly, "it's being here, next to you."

A lump lodges in my throat. I swallow roughly, but the stubborn thing remains. My voice thick with recent sleep—and not emotion, damn it—I say, "You're adorable, you know that?"

He shrugs, a sly smile curving his lips. "Now that you are awake, my Shannon, I want to show you something."

This isn't the first time Mal's wanted to show me something when I first wake up. Sometimes I like my surprises—like when he drew that chalk drawing of me after our first night, or when he figured out how to use my old coffee pot that had been in a cabinet for two years—and sometimes I wonder how

I slept through it—like when he tried to cook foil-covered leftovers in my microwave and nearly started a fire.

I hope this is a good one.

Mal leads me to the living room, covering my eyes with his massive hands while guiding me out of my bedroom. Everything smells okay, and though I can't see anything, light filters in through the cracks of his ginormous fingers. We still have electricity, unlike the microwave fiasco. Mal got lucky that day. The power had shorted, taking out the lights before the whole appliance had a chance to explode.

"What is it?" I ask, impatient as ever. "I want to see."

"And so you shall. Look."

Mal removes his hands.

"Oh."

Oh is right. Looks like, after I went to sleep, my monster decided to explore his gift a little more. Using one of the larger canvases propped up on a makeshift easel, he filled the entire canvas with—you guessed it—a full portrait of me.

If anything, it's even more gorgeous than the first time he drew my face.

"First your chalk drawings, now this? Am I the only thing you know how to draw?"

I meant it as a tease. Good ol' Shannon, with the defense mechanism that turns her into a complete smart ass when she can't handle her emotions.

And then there's Mal. My opposite in so many ways. Physically *and* emotionally.

He settles his big hands on my shoulders. "You are my inspiration, my Shannon. My muse. When all else pales in comparison, it would be a waste of your generosity to paint anything other than you."

I don't know what to say that that so I simply continue to look at the brushstrokes on the painting.

Honestly, it would be so easy to believe that all he wants from me is sex—but then he says something like that and I know I'm only fooling myself. Mal wants me for me. Sure, the sex is definitely a perk, and I'll never see him complaining, but he wants a companion. His muse. I have his essence now. I know him in ways that I don't really understand yet, but even if I didn't, I would know he was a lonely demon back in Sombra.

No wonder he grabbed on tight with both hands when he met me. If I spent my whole life—if I spent *a thousand years*—being told there was one single soul out there for me, one I could experience love and life and happiness with, wouldn't I yearn for it? And when it was in front of me, wouldn't I do anything to keep it?

Which leaves me to wonder: what will I do to keep him? And will I figure that out before our looming deadline?

Good questions. Too bad I don't have the answers.

CHAPTER 19
TURN THE PAGE

SHANNON

Later that day, my phone rings. Though it's not programmed as one of my contacts, something about the number is familiar.

As I'm about to answer, I realize something. Derek never called. He smiled and waved at me the last time I saw him at The Beanery on Thursday, but that's the only time I went this week—and Derek never called.

The old Shannon would've been butthurt about that. He was gorgeous, and I would've loved to take him up on that offer for dinner. But that was the old Shannon.

The new Shannon is trying to justify falling for a demonic shadow monster after knowing him for only a week.

I shove that thought out of my head, swiping my

phone with a little more force than the act calls for. Urging myself to calm the heck down, I take a deep breath, then say, "Hello?"

"Hi. Is this Shannon?"

"Sure is," I chirp. "How can I help?"

"This is Kennedy. Kennedy Barnes. From Turn the Page? When I stopped in to get my coffee this morning, Derek gave me your number and said you were looking for me?"

Okay. Next time I stop by The Beanery for a little treat, I'm so gonna drop a twenty in his tip jar. Even though I got most of the answers I needed from Amy, I'm still grateful he passed along my message and my phone number to Kennedy at least.

"Oh my god, Kennedy! Yes. I… how was your vacation?"

"Something I needed desperately. Lord knows I missed my store, but it was nice to have a week to myself. But I'm sure that's not what you wanted to talk to me about, so, please. What can I do for you?"

Right to it, then, huh? "It's about a book."

Kennedy's laugh is so soft and sweet, it's closer to a giggle. "Usually is."

Right. Because she's a bookseller. "Do you remember a couple of weeks ago? When you convinced me to buy that leather-bound book with the pentacle on the cover?"

"The one you were convinced was a spellbook?"

It had a pentacle embossed in the leather. Anyone would think it was a spellbook. "That's the one."

"Kinda. Why? Did you change your mind? Because I guess I could buy it back from you as long as it's in the same condition it left my shop in."

"Oh, no. No. That's not why I'm calling," I say hurriedly. "I don't want to get rid of the book."

I still need it. Since Mal gave me his essence and I know Sombran now, I've been slowly working my way through the book, checking to see what other spells it holds. I haven't had that much time—and I get a headache when I read Sombran since I see the words in Mal's language and in English at the same time instead of an instant translation—but, so far, the grimoire is kind of a dud. The true love spell is the only one that seems like a real spell. There are also poems and stories, recipes and Sombran history, but nothing else that reads like the *verus amor* spell that brought Mal to me.

"I'm glad, Shannon. But if it isn't a return you want, how else can I help you?"

Last Saturday, I hoped she'd be able to tell me where she got this book from. For all the times I've meandered around her store, looking for another book I could curl up with and read, I've gotten to know how Kennedy runs her business a bit. A lot of her books come from donations, estate sales, and when a library culls its stacks. The spellbook had been a new arrival the day I bought it off of her, and I had the idea that, maybe if I knew how it ended up in Turn the Page, it might help me figure out what to do with Mal.

That was a week ago. What a difference a week makes. Instead of trying to banish Mal, I'm thinking about whether or not I can keep him. Kennedy can't help with that, but that doesn't mean she can't tell me where the book came from anyway.

For Amy's sake, I'd like to know. She'd been so surprised to learn that it ended up in a used book store in Jericho, where it then fell into the hands of someone who was fated to meet—and maybe mate— a Sombra demon.

Just like her.

"I was wondering, do you know where you got it from? How it became part of your stock in the first place?"

Kennedy is quiet for a moment, as though she's trying to remember. "Honestly, I'm not sure. I remember that I had gotten an unusually large ship-ment that day from at least three different vendors."

"Oh." Crap. I mean, it was a long shot, but I figured it couldn't hurt to ask. "Thanks anyway."

"If you want, bring it by the shop. If I input it into the system before I sold it to you, it'll have a SKU that might track its source. Not saying it will… sometimes I sell out-of-print titles under a dummy, but I can check for you."

"Really?"

"Sure. I'm here 'til seven tonight, and I open at nine tomorrow. Come by whenever."

"Thanks, Kennedy. I will."

It wasn't a guarantee. It might even be a waste of time. But as much as I'm curious for Amy's sake, I've gotta admit that it does seem real coincidental that the spellbook found its way to me in time for me to find Mal.

He calls it Fate. Me… I wish I could believe that.

Just like I wish I could believe that things could stay the way they are forever.

They could. As I finish my call with Kennedy, I have to admit that they could. All it would take is me accepting Mal's claim. Mate the monster, and nothing would have to change.

Well. No. That's being both obtuse and naive. *Everything* would change. Mal would be mine forever, and considering the fact that he's immortal—and mating him would make me immortal, too—I don't use that word lightly. With Sombra demons, there is no divorce. There is no space. There is no "whoops, I changed my mind". We'd be permanently tied together in a mate bond that I still don't really understand, but that even Amy insists existed.

But, on a day-to-day basis, nothing would have to change for a while. I could still go to work, and now that we've figured out the whole "essence" thing, I won't have to worry about getting "sick" again. I could teach him more recipes, and he could help me when I forget about cleaning my apartment. And, despite our differences, we've proved so far that we're compatible in the bedroom. True, we haven't had penetrative sex so far, but nothing else has been off-limits.

And, gotta admit, I've never been more satisfied with any of my previous lovers…

He's watching me. Mal's always watching me, but as I stand there with my phone in my hand, I see the look on his face and remember with a jolt that he probably has a good idea that I'm wavering. He knows me, after all.

He probably knows I'm itching to give in to him.

But he's not pushing. I'll give Mal that. Though I know that there isn't anything he wants more than to call me his and have me accept that claim, he hasn't pushed me to choose him since the beginning. Once he understood that mate bonds—and lifelong matings —don't work the same for humans as they do demons, he backed off. He gave me the space I so desperately needed, even when we could only stay a few feet apart.

Is it any wonder that I'm actually mulling the idea of a future with Mal over like this?

I slip my phone into my back pocket. "That was the chick who sold me the spellbook. You up for a visit to her store?"

"With you, my Shannon? Always."

It isn't until I'm locking the door behind us that it

dawns on me that I never even thought about convincing him to stay behind.

"So?" I ask a touch impatiently. "What do you think?"

Kennedy is a couple of years older than me. With a heart-shaped face, dirty blonde hair that falls in soft curls, and pretty hazel eyes, she looks extremely innocent and gentle. Her voice is soft and sweet, and she has these high cheekbones that make it seem like she's always smiling. Even now, as she frowns as she looks over the spellbook, I can't help but think of the bookseller as impish.

As I wait for her answer, Mal trails his shadowy hand across my back. As the slight heat withdraws, I know that he's moved away from me.

He probably wants to look around the bookstore. Turn the Page is a lot for first-timers. Instead of rows and rows of bookshelves with neatly organized stock, Kennedy has a system of her own. She has racks and rows, piles and bins full of every kind of book you can imagine.

Including spellbooks, it seems.

"I'm sorry, Shannon, but I guess I sold this to you before I put it in the system."

Crap. I was hoping she wouldn't say that.

"But," she adds, giving me a little hope, "if you

want to leave this behind with me, I can make a couple of calls, show it to some members of a group I belong to. Someone might recognize it, and if not, I can see if I have anything else like it in my inventory."

I highly doubt that.

"Um. Yeah. If it'll help, that's okay with me."

"It won't be long. Maybe a week or two? Then I'll have this right back to you."

"Okay."

"And," Kennedy adds, lowering the spellbook to her counter, "if you want to look around, I've gotten a big box of romance novels in since the last time I saw you. Even got some indies featured on the endcap. I know you enjoy those."

"Sure. I'll do that."

I make a move away from the counter when, out of nowhere, it hits me that my demon isn't anywhere nearby.

I pause.

Hang on. Where is Mal?

I thought he was looking around, but I get the feeling that he's not even in the store anymore. I don't even sense him close to me, and considering he's basically been my second shadow this whole last week, I'm not a big fan of suddenly being alone like this.

Glancing behind me, I see that the door to Turn the Page is open. That's right. A beautiful May day, Kennedy had left it open to get some fresh air.

Which means that Mal could've disappeared right through it and I never would've known it.

There are some limits to being a shadow. He's not a ghost. He can't float through walls, even if he can make the edges of his body transparent. It's like his claws or his cock. He can turn them to shadow, but they still exist. The closer to his middle, the more solid he is, even when he's in his faded form. In order to leave, he'd need a door or a window. Some kind of opening.

But why would he leave me?

I'm distracted. I know I am. After I take a quick tour through the store, verifying that Mal is gone, I return to the counter empty-handed. I'm barely listening as Kennedy is telling me about a couple of estate sales she might've gotten the spellbook from. I nod absently, but my mind is stuck on Mal.

Finally, I can't take it anymore. After thanking her for her time, and asking her to let me know when she calls in her contacts and finds out more about the spellbook, I make my escape.

Mal isn't waiting outside for me on Main Street. However, if I concentrate, I can kind of pick up on his essence. No time for second-guessing my instincts. I follow the tug low in my belly until I've gone a block down from Turn the Page, hitting the break between one street and the next.

I know this spot. It's the darkened alley with the closed-off end where Mal and me hid from that green-eyed demon from his world. Now, like the other day, the narrow way is full of shadows.

But that's not all.

With a gasp, I break for the far end.

There are three demons surrounding Mal. One is the green-eyed demon. Glaine. I don't recognize the other two, but each one is in his shadow form: black skin, arching horns, golden runes dancing over their brawny arms, and glowing eyes. The one on the left has eyes the same shade as Mal, while the final demon has dark purple eyes.

I know my monster's silhouette. He's matched them, also wearing his inky black shadow form, his body hunched as he faces off against the other demons.

As though he can sense me coming, he spins around to face me.

And that's when I see that Mal is wearing a length of chains. Manacles clasp each of his wrists, glowing chains connecting them.

My demon looks pained.

"Shannon." His voice is a ragged whisper. "You have to go. Leave me."

No way in fucking hell.

"Mal? What's going on here?"

The three demons don't look surprised to see me. In fact, I get the idea that they were waiting for me. Like this is some kind of trap.

It's too late for Mal to hide me in his shadows like

he did before. With three intimidating, glowing gazes watching my every move, I can't pretend like they don't see me.

Welp. Better make the best of it.

"You." I point at the green-eyed demon. Since he was the one who threatened Mal with the chains the last time he was here, I figure he's the big shot in charge. "What do you think you're doing? Get those chains off of him *now*."

"I can't. It's the night of the gold moon," Glaine announces with a huff. "Malphas has failed to make the mortal his. He is now in breach of Duke Haures's first law. No mortal shall know of Sombra unless they're a mate."

I don't understand. That makes no sense. "I *am* his mate."

"No," rumbles Mal. His expression is flat, but his eyes are wild. "She's not. Glaine is right. She didn't choose me. I deserve the chains, but she doesn't."

Glaine throws Mal a look of pure disdain. "She's also in breach. You must know we can't leave the mortal here to tell stories of Sombra. She has your essence. She knows your secrets, and ours. That can't stand." He snaps his fingers, calling the attention of the demon to his right. "Prepare chains for the mortal, too."

"No! Leave her!"

Glaine ignores Mal's roar. "Now, Sammael."

Did I think his eyes were wild before? The bright

golden color turns almost white with the force of his glow as he fights against the angry orangey-red chains. "Leave her be, I said!"

While Glaine rearranges his features in a smirk, and Sammael starts to conjure another length of chains between his palms, the third demon clears his throat.

Glaine's head shoots his way. "Not now, Apollyon."

The third demon—Apollyon—ignores him. "Malphas. You know what you have to do."

"What?" I demand. If there's some way to stop this, I'm for Mal doing *anything*. "What is it?"

An inner battle plays out across his face. Mal is breathing heavily, his chest rising and falling as his suddenly dim gaze locks on me. "My Shannon… forgive me. I never wanted to do this, but my clan leader is right. I won't let them punish you, and it's selfish to keep our bond when it will never be finalized. Our time's run out. I can't let them chain you."

"You're making me nervous," I say to Mal. "What… what's going on?"

He takes in a deep breath, shuddering it out. "I release you."

It's like an anchor that has kept me tethered even without me knowing. Once Mal cuts the tie between us, I start to drift away. I don't think I noticed how much of him had taken root inside of me—inside of my soul—until he severed our bond on his side.

I grab hold of it with two hands.

I'm not going to let him go. If the choice is Mal or no Mal, impulsive Shannon is gonna finally make it.

"No!" I blurt out. "He's mine!"

Glaine gives me a withering look. "Malphas is Duke Haures's to punish. Know your place."

Punish? Oh, *heck*, no.

I race forward, jumping in front of him. Even with my arms thrown out wide, I barely cover his bulk, but I try anyway. "No one is punishing Mal."

"Mal?" echoes Sammael. He sniffs as he addresses my demon. "You let the mortal disrespect you this way, Malphas?"

"I use the name my mate chose for me," grates Mal. "And you disrespect my Shannon by refusing to acknowledge her claim to me even if I have to let her go."

"That's right." I jerk my thumb behind me, glaring at the trio of shadowy shapes. "This is my monster. I mean, my mate. And I'm not going anywhere. You guys can't have him."

MALPHAS

Nox willingly accepted his chains. When he attempted to explain his motivations, I still couldn't understand why he would do that —until Glaine, Sammael, and Apollyon came for me.

I sensed them before Shannon did. With the two soldiers—and my clan leader—arriving just ahead of the gold moon, their power was increased. Their portal opened much faster than it had when it was just Glaine, and I was able to slip out of the bookstore without Shannon knowing how much danger she was in.

To protect her, I held my hands out for the chain. For the sake of my mate, I let Sammael conjure them and place them around my wrists because I hoped that they'd drag me away before Shannon came looking for me.

I was too late.

Just as I prepared myself to say goodbye, she came dashing around the corner, her fair hair streaming behind her. She froze when she realized that Duke Haures had sent three soldiers after me this time, and my mind went from already mourning her to trying to figure out how I could save her from my fate.

Even if the gold chains didn't contain my ability to wield my shadows, I couldn't use them to shield her when the other demons saw her coming for me. I could pretend she wasn't my mate, but it wouldn't matter. Humans aren't allowed to set eyes upon a Sombra demon, and my Shannon saw *four*.

Just then, it was all about saving her. Only... to my absolute amazement, my little mortal decided she was going to save *me*.

She claimed me. In front of three other demons, she called me hers.

She said they can't have me.

I inch around her. While I appreciate what she's doing, no honorable male will stand back and let his much more delicate mate stand between him and three enemies. I might be chained, but that won't stop me if they try to put chains on Shannon next.

Nox broke through them. So can I.

But I don't have to. Before Sammael could finish conjuring the chains, Apollyon steps forward.

"There is still time until the gold moon finishes its ascent," he announces. "If the mortal means what she says, we must give Malphas the chance to bond his mate to him."

Shannon dances in front of me again. "You're going to let him go? Take the chains off and we can leave?"

Apollyon's purple eyes flicker. "As long as he's a mated male by the time the gold moon rises completely, he's broken no law."

"So, let me get this straight… if I go home and fuck Mal, that makes him my mate. I gotta do it soon, though, because of some arbitrary deadline that you believe in. Something about Mal going demonic? Okay. Sounds fake 'cause Mal is, like, the opposite of a demon, but whatever. Sex, and then you guys can butt out of our business, okay?"

Have I ever been more enamored with another soul in my life?

"My mate," I breathe out in amazement.

She looks up at me, her lips quirked in a sly grin. "Amy explained some of the basics to me, big guy. I know there's a little Sombra demon mojo behind the scenes, but that's the gist of it, right?"

She is correct. "Yes. I gave you most of my essence that day in the shadows, but if we mate and my essence goes inside of you, there's no breaking our bond."

"And, what? This duke will know that?"

"He has ways," offers Apollyon. "He'll know, and as long as Malphas keeps out of sight of every other mortal, he can stay here if he chooses."

I hold my breath. Will my Shannon accept me into her home as readily as she will her body? This last week, she's been determined to find a way to send me back to Sombra. Has that changed?

I fervently hope so.

"Not a big fan of knowing you guys are all involved in my sex life, but it is what it is." Shannon shrugs. "And Amy says we can go to Sombra if we want to eventually so if I get bored of hiding my mate, that's always an idea."

Mi uxor.

She's speaking in Sombran. With my essence flooding through her, she probably doesn't even realize that she instinctively addressed the other demons in a tongue they would understand.

My heart soars. In front of Glaine, Sammael, and Apollyon, she fully claimed me as hers. And when we return to her home, and I finally give her the last of my essence, I will truly be her mate. And she's even entertaining the idea of visiting my home plane.

Yes!

I hold out my wrists.

Sammael scowls.

Apollyon nods.

Glaine sighs.

"Sammael? Remove the chains. Apollyon is right. Malphas has a few hours more before the gold moon fully rises. But," he says, looking directly at me, "if the bond is not finalized by then, Duke Haures will send us back."

Shannon smiles sweetly at them. "Keep in mind you'll probably get an eyeful of Mal's dick if you do. Because we're going to be mating all night long."

A male can only hope.

SHANNON INSISTS ON RETURNING TO HER APARTMENT. If she'd allow me to mount her in front of the others just to prove that she was mine, I would've done so gladly, but I discover that that is one more difference between mortals and Sombra demons. She requires some element of privacy, and I will always give her whatever she desires.

I remember how she once suggested I pick her up and carry her and offered to do that now to cut the trip short. Laughing, she points out that everything we did would've been for nothing if another human noticed that a demon was running down Main Street. I then offer to melt into the shadows with her, but she just shakes her head.

Her quarters aren't that far. To me, it seems like I'm crossing the lengths of Sombra before we arrive at her front door. I'm whipping around in my faded shadow form, buzzing near her feet where no human would notice me.

Down the hall, a door begins to open. I know without seeing who it is that it'll be that older female who is too concerned with Shannon. I murmur for her to hurry so that she can avoid facing the dreaded Mrs. Winslow.

Luckily, she pops open her door before the other female can call out to her. Immediately materializing in my demon form, I reach around Shannon and lock the front door for her. Then, so aroused that I'm not sure I'll be able to hold back until I work my cock inside of her, I throw Shannon over my shoulder and race for the bedroom.

Again, she laughs. "You really want to do this, don't you, Mal?"

I will never lie to my mate.

After I lay her gently down on her bed, I tell her, "I've dreamed of this for my entire life. From the moment I knew that Fate would reward me with a female, I waited for the one who would be mine. And now that I have you, and you've pledged yourself to me in front of others, I want to bond you to me before something else comes between us."

She raises her eyebrows, teasingly sticking the tip of her tongue out from between her lips. Her hands tap the rough coverings on her legs. "My jeans are between us."

Not for long.

Flexing my hands, revealing my demon claws, I make quick work of her jeans. I don't leave a single scratch on my mate's porcelain skin, but her coverings? They're mere shreds by the time I'm done.

"Oh my fucking god, Mal. I mean, those jeans weren't cheap, but that was so hot, I don't give a shit."

I pleased her?

I lift my claws again.

She holds out her hands. "Wait. I like these panties. Don't shred them, okay?"

My chest is heaving, but still I bow my head. "As you wish."

"Just for that, I'm gonna make this real good for you."

As if I wouldn't like anything she did to me…

Shannon hurriedly tugs off her panties, tossing them somewhere off to the side. Just as quickly, she removes her shirt, then her breast covering. Once she's bared to me, I realize that I still have on the shadows that conceal my cock.

Before my next breath, it's gone.

My mate's eyes widen for a heartbeat as she locks on my erection. I'm hard as stone, the head almost reaching for her, as if my cock has a mind of its own. It knows exactly where it belongs.

So long as Shannon doesn't change her mind, that is.

"Shannon." I have to spit out her name through gritted teeth. "Are you still willing to mate with me?

To take my essence, and complete this bond so that we'll be together for the rest of time?"

For a few terrifying seconds, she's quiet. I'm almost convinced that she did change her mind—and then she nods.

"But, uh, you remember how you make your dick go a little smaller when I want to play with it?" At my nod, she adds, "You can do that to get it inside of me, right? So we'll fit?"

I realize then that her fear—that, because of our size difference, we wouldn't be compatible—has been one of the biggest obstacles between us, even if she never came out and said so. And maybe I should've explained that I would've done anything to ensure she could take me, including transforming to shadow so that it would fit snugly inside of her.

But I don't have to.

"Oh, my mate," I purr. I climb up on the bed, going to all fours. My cock is leading the way to her as Shannon falls back, spreading her legs. A tinge of nerves colors her scent, but it's nothing compared to the lust that fills the air. "I thought you spoke to Nox's mate about what it is to belong to a Sombra demon."

She juts out her chin in absolute defiance—while still surrendering her body completely to me. "I did. I just… she said it would work, and I figured she was talking about you turning to shadow."

I grip Shannon by her hips, positioning her perfectly for me. Her breathing turns shallow as I take my shaft in one hand. The other? I dip my finger—with a shadow for a claw—into her pussy, making sure she's ready to take me. We'd decided that we were cutting it too close to the deadline for foreplay, and by the time we arrived at her apartment, I thought we were both as ready to mate as we would ever be. Now that I've proven it, it's time to bond Shannon to me.

"Didn't you wonder why it's so important to share our essences?"

She shifts a little as I put the blunt tip of my cock against her opening. "Honestly," she pants out, "I thought it was because it would make me want you. You said it was so I could hide in the shadows, but I… I wasn't sure. But lately…"

I push a little, getting the head wedged inside of her tight little body. "Lately, my mate?"

She moans, then says, "Not your mate. Not… not yet."

"Ah. But you will be." I tilt my hips, easing another inch inside of her. Her white skin with its blonde curls welcomes my near-purple cock. I almost spill from that sight alone. "Once you accept the rest of my essence, we'll never be separated.

"As for the first bit that I shared with you," I add, thrusting inside of her with one last rough shove, seating myself entirely inside of Shannon, "my essence primes my mate for me. No matter how big a male, or small a female, with our mingled essences, we will always fit."

Shannon gasps. At first, I think it's because of how full she feels to have my entire cock stuffed inside of her. It is quite impressive, even for a Sombra male, I must say. We fit, though it's still snug, and I want to give her a moment to get used to me.

But then she lifts her back off of the mattress, smacking me in the chest. "You asshole! You couldn't have told me that days ago? Ugh!" With a frustrated grunt, she lets herself fall back on the bed, her eyes closed.

"Shannon? My mate? Are you okay?"

She quirks one open. "I would be if my mate decided to stop staring at me and started to freaking move already. Come on, Mal. Fuck me. Mate me. Make me yours, and then we're going to talk about the things that Shannon should probably be told." Her eyes shut again. "Essence, seriously?"

I smile. How could I forget? This is Shannon, after all. My human mate.

Who says mating to create a bond for life has to be serious?

I pull out just enough to have the leverage to thrust back in.

And I smile. "As ever, my mate, your wish is my command."

———

I've always known I would love my mate. When I was fortunate enough to find her, I would treat her like she deserved. I would love her and revere her and make her the queen of our own little world.

And then I was summoned by my wee mortal mate and all of my plans for the future changed in a blink of her lovely sky-blue eyes.

Her eyes are closed right now. I can tell from the rise and fall of her beautiful breasts that she's not quite asleep, though she's nearly there.

Masculine pride puffs out my chest. I've never mated fully before—of course not, because I never knew Shannon before—but she has. Of course, she would never compare me to her previous lovers, a fact that I'm grateful for, but when we finished our second mating, she patted me on the chest and said she was sure she made the right choice.

It was music to my ears.

I'm still wide awake. My body is tired, but my mind is whirling. I don't want to miss a single moment of the beginning of our new bonded life together.

I stroke Shannon's sunflower marking reverentially. My claws are halfway formed, enough for me to revel at the soft touch of her skin while making sure I don't exactly scratch her.

"You really like my ink, don't you, Mal?" she murmurs sleepily.

Of course. It's beautiful, just like my mate, but her sunflower is special to me. When I see it, I remember

Jurissa's vision of my future. A mate who blooms in the sun, and who is full to the brim of magic and life.

That's my Shannon in one.

Already we've mated twice. The first time, I climaxed almost immediately. Feeling her tight pussy envelope my entire shaft was too much. After only a few strokes, I went off, filling her with every bit of essence I stored up in my sack.

Shannon didn't mind. The sooner, the better, she said, reminding me that we were mating on borrowed time. But once we got the first mating out of the way —our bond snapping into place as soon as I erupted inside of her—she said the next one was ours.

And, using some "tips" and "tricks" she learned from Amy, I lasted much, much longer. By the end of our mating, Shannon was mewling beneath me, my hair was plastered to my scalp from sweat, and I couldn't believe that I'd gone an age without such pleasure in my life.

Even more amazing? I have an eternity of mating Shannon to look forward to.

Hours have passed. Neither one of us has mentioned it, but every now and then Shannon would glance over to the corner where she'd drawn the star shape in chalk all those days ago, just to see if a portal would appear.

It's not there anymore. She'd mopped up the salt and chalk two nights ago while I was dozing after she worked magic on me with her mouth. I never remarked on that, though I did notice she left my portrait of her on the floor.

Did I wonder if she'd warmed up to me when she erased the chalk drawing that trapped me in her quarters that first night? Of course. But until Shannon claimed me in front of Duke Haures's soldiers, it was only a hope.

But now she's mine.

Forever.

She smiles into my chest. "You like when I touch you even more than my ink."

"I love everything about you." Leaning over her, I nuzzle her pale hair. "Because it's you, and I love you, my mate."

Shannon sucks in a breath. Lifting her head up so that I can look into her beautiful face, I see her eyes are wide.

"What?"

"I just… I knew you wanted me. And I knew you cared. But I guess I didn't think—"

Ah. "That I loved you, my Shannon?"

She nods.

I nip at her bottom lip, careful not to cut her with my fangs. "I've lived a thousand years. Longer even. But I wasn't truly alive until you lit up my life. I might be made of shadows, but I needed something bright. I needed *you*."

"Yeah?" She snuggles closer, holding me tight. "Good thing, big guy, because I'm not going anywhere. And neither are you. Not unless we go together."

"Together," I rumble. "I like the sound of that."

Together.

Forever.

Just like we were meant to be.

SHANNON

Okay.

Shadow dick.

Let me tell you. It's... *wow.*

Ten out of ten. I'd definitely recommend it.

Well, if you have your own Sombra mate, I would. Not Mal. My seven-foot monster is all mine, from the tippy tops of his demon horns to the massive feet that just goes to prove that there's some truth to the saying about shoe size and penises.

He's mine, thank you, and now that we're fully mated, I have no intention of sharing.

As if he'd let me. If I thought he was devoted to me before our mate bond was finalized, that's nothing compared to how he acts after we did the deed. In fact, I woke up a few hours later, a little sore but absolutely cozy as I felt the tips of his claws gently threading through my messy hair. He'd tucked me against his side, one arm over my belly, the other serving as a pillow. My head was on his bicep, his catcher mitt of a hand cradling the side of my skull as he, well, petted me.

When he saw I was awake, he gave me a small smile with the tips of his fangs peeking out before he murmured, "Rest, my mate. I have you."

Mal does. He really does. He was willing to go back to Sombra in chains if that's what I wanted, and now that I've claimed him as mine, he is willing to live a secret life with me in my world where the most he can be is my shadow. Whatever I want, he'll willingly give it to me.

Like he said when I first summoned him, my wish is his command. He's no genie, but he's even better. He's my demon mate, my beloved monster, and for the first time in my life, my impulsiveness doesn't seem so reckless.

In fact, my decision to bond myself to Mal so soon… it seems right. From the moment I woke up to that chalk portrait of me on my floor, me falling for him was probably inevitable. Sharing our essence sped up the process, so did the timeline of the gold moon, but once I was more intrigued by Mal than scared of him, I think we both knew we'd end up mating.

Heck, Mal knew from the moment I summoned him to my world. I was his mate as soon as he saw me. It just took me a little longer to catch up.

Still, because I'm me, I keep waiting for it to hit me. To *really* hit me. I don't ever second-guess my decisions, though sometimes I have to admit I might've made a mistake. The sex the first two or three days after our bonding kind of keeps me too occupied to dwell on how much my life has changed —and I don't only mean because mating Mal means I'm basically immortal myself, too, now—but as powerful as Mal's shadow dick is, eventually I have to face what exactly we've done.

Being intimate with Mal was one thing, but now that we've gone all the way? I'm his as much as he's mine. No need for a human wedding since I already made my vows to him; even if I had no idea what I was saying the night I summoned Mal to me, I gave myself up to him completely when we mated. The mate bond is complete between us, and nothing can separate us now except for his unlikely death—and, now that my lifespan is tied irrevocably to his, I'll follow Mal even then.

Talk about impulsive. In the matter of a week or so, I went from summoning a monster, to fooling around with him, to accepting my place at his side. Whether we stay in my world like he's offered me or go visit Sombra now that a portal will finally open up to us, it doesn't matter. Wherever we go, we'll be together.

For now, we're sticking around Jericho. Just because I took Mal as my mate doesn't mean that I'm ready to change everything about my life. I'm only twenty-nine. I've worked hard for my apartment and my job, and though I could live to be a thousand-and-twenty-nine easily—and isn't that a heavy notion?—I'll only have this one "mortal" lifetime. I like my friends. I like my home. My job… well, I like my colleagues and most of my clients, so that has to count for something. Right?

In between frequent bouts of getting it on, I discuss our future with my new mate. Mal eventually wants to return to his own plane, but he's more than happy to give me a couple of decades here on Earth first. I might never be able to walk around with him, holding hands and showing him off to my neighbors, but my mate is talented, gentle, generous, protective, and hot as heck. For our mating to work, we both will have to make some sacrifices, but I'm sure it'll be worth it.

Besides, I like the idea of keeping Mal just for me.

And then there's Amy. With her and Nox only a couple of hours away, it's nice to have someone who understands what it's like to have a Sombra demon for a mate. After I called my boss and told her I was taking another week PTO—she thinks I'm still recovering, while I decided it counts as a honeymoon—I texted Amy and let her know that me and Mal are a sure thing. She congratulated us and offered to host a dinner in our honor.

We're going on Saturday. I'm actually looking forward to it, even if I had to… convince Mal that it'll be worth it to have one day where we're not cozying up in my bed.

The day before we're going out to see Amy and Nox, she sends me another message. Since we're heading to her place for dinner, she wanted to know if I could bring the spellbook with me. Of course I told her I would.

There was no way to refuse. If it wasn't for nine-year-old Amy scrawling her name on the inner cover, I never would've met her in the first place. With the mystery of her aunt's disappearance still weighing on her, if I could give her Susanna's book, I would.

Only one problem. I left it with Kennedy last Saturday, and with everything that has happened since, I never returned to Turn the Page to pick it up. She didn't call me, either, but it's been a week. I'm ready to take it back.

Now that our mate bond is complete and we don't have to worry about the duke's soldiers ambushing us again, there's no reason why Mal and I have to stick together like velcro anymore. Rolling out of bed, heading toward my dresser for a change of clothes, I tell Mal that I'm going to run down to the bookstore and get the book back from Kennedy. Considering I left him spent and panting after I had some fun with him, I thought he'd want to stay behind.

I should've known better. Mal doesn't have to follow me around like a shadow, but he *wants* to. And who am I to tell him no? So long as he goes from his demon form to shadow, I don't mind.

Not because I really give a shit what he looks like. He's a monster, but he's *my* monster. I've grown to appreciate his red skin and his glowing golden eyes. Gotta love the way his gleaming horns give me leverage while I'm sitting on his face, and his size… he makes me feel both protected and adored when he wraps me in his embrace.

Though I'd love to see how Mrs. Winslow and some of my other neighbors would react to his demonic appearance, I have to remember that the rest of the human world probably isn't ready to discover there are Sombra demons who can cross planes. I mean, way too many of us can't handle other humans we think of as different. How the heck would they treat Mal?

Plus, those other demons made it clear. Mal can stay with me once we bonded, but their duke's law stands. If any mortal—besides me and Amy for obvious reasons—sees Mal, our time on Earth is over. There might even be chains in the future for us.

No, thanks.

Good thing we've learned how to walk down Main Street together, me seemingly by myself, Mal the shadow at my back. Doesn't matter that I try to insist that I don't need him to come with me, I'm pleased when he murmurs that at my side is where he belongs.

We go together. My sweet mate even offers to accompany me into The Beanery for a latte, though I shake him off. Maybe later. Right now? I want to grab the book, then go back to the apartment with Mal. Come Monday, our new life will have to begin: with me going back to work, and Mal getting the chance to really explore all the painting supplies I ordered for him. This is our honeymoon. If it wasn't for Amy's request, I wouldn't have crawled out of our bedroom until tomorrow afternoon.

It should be an in and out type of sitch. Kennedy's been back from her vacation for about a week now, and I checked her hours the last time I was here. Turn the Page is open until seven pm. It's only three. There's no reason she won't be there.

Tell that to the locked door and the darkened store.

What?

Because I can't believe that Turn the Page is closed again, I rattle the knob. Nope. Definitely locked.

Shielding my eyes with my hands, I press my nose against the glass. All of the lights inside of the shop are turned off, except for a few emergency lights. Using the faint yellow glow, I peek inside, but the store is empty. Kennedy isn't there.

I frown. Did she close up for a late lunch or something? I'd passed by her shop a few times when it was shut for her to get some food, but usually Kennedy would leave the lights on and a note on the door that said she'd be back soon.

Glancing at the door, I see the hours posted— which proves that she *should* be open—and that's all. No other note.

No Kennedy.

No spellbook.

Huh. Well, that was a waste of a trip.

"Looks like we struck out," I mutter. "She's not here."

As I step away from the closed bookstore, I feel a breeze against the back of my neck. My hair flutters, but not from the wind. My shadowy mate has slid out of the alley, caressing my arm, my neck, my cheek. With the sun shining brightly, he's barely a flicker, but even if I can't really make him out, I can *sense* him.

My boobs are suddenly super heavy. My nipples go hard, poking through my tank. Lust rushes through me, but it's not only mine. Now that we're fully bonded, it isn't just his essence that I feel. Through our mate bond, my body reacts to his.

And my mate is hungering for me.

I chuckle, lifting my hand. Warm air brushes against my fingers as the edge of Mal's shadowy form floats through it. It's as close as I can get to touching him when we're out in public, but with his need making me hot and ready, I instinctively reach for him.

"Already?" I murmur, low enough that only he can hear me. "Didn't I tire you out before we left the apartment?"

"Never, my mate," comes Mal's husky whisper. "I'll never be tired of you."

"Good. I'm gonna hold you to that."

"Mm. So long as I get to hold you."

He caresses me again, and I shiver. Hold me? Yeah. That sounds great.

I glance back at Turn the Page. Next time Kennedy's in, I'll get the book for Amy. Until then, I have an entire weekend to look forward to before I have to go back to work on Monday, and a mate who wants me more than his next breath.

So he has horns. So he's technically a demon. So he comes from a whole other plane.

He's Malphas, he's a monster, and he's *mine*.

THAT'S IT FOR SHANNON AND MAL'S STORY! IF YOU'RE interested in learning more about Amy and Nox, their story will be told next in *Stolen by the Shadows*, coming soon! Keep reading/scrolling/clicking for information about their book—as well as a special offer for fans of this book!

Shannon & Mal

MATED TO THE MONSTER

KEEP IN TOUCH

Stay tuned for what's coming up next! Follow me at any of these places — or sign up for my newsletter — for news, promotions, upcoming releases, and more:

>> Newsletter <<

AVAILABLE NOW

STOLEN BY THE SHADOWS

What if your imaginary friend was *real*?

Then again, Nox was never as imaginary as he was supposed to be, and while I thought of him as my friend, he watched over me because he knew we were meant to be more than that.

He knew that we were *fated*.

Me? I had no freaking clue, but that made sense. The last time I saw him I was twelve. He was the shadow monster that kept me safe. But, like all imaginary friends, he was just gone one day. And, as I grew up, I forgot all about Nox.

He never forgot about me.

Fifteen years later and he's still as much a protector as he always was. When I'm stalked by an ex who just can't accept that we're over, Connor isn't the only one who likes to hide in the shadows. Too bad for him that Nox *is* the shadows.

He's changed, though. My old imaginary friend is wrapped in golden chains, his shape unlike any he ever showed me before. He's big, and he's fierce, and he saves me from Connor only to take me for himself.

And I... I'm kind of okay with that.

---

* *Stolen by the Shadows* is the second book in the **Sombra Demons** series. It tells the story of Amy and Nox, the bonded couple introduced in *Mated to the Monster*.

Releasing October 25, 2022!

AVAILABLE NOW

NEVER HIS MATE

After my mate rejected me, I wanted to kill him. Instead, I ran away— which nearly killed *me*...

A year ago, everything was different. I had just left my home, joining the infamous Mountainside Pack. The daughter of an omega wolf, I've always been prized -- but just not as prized as I would be if my new packmates found out my secret.

But then my fated mate—Mountainside's Alpha—rejects me in front of his whole pack council and my secret gets out, I realize I only have one option. Going lone wolf is the only choice I've got, and I take it.

Now I live in Muncie, hiding in plain sight. If the

wolves ever left the mountains surrounding the city, I'd be in big trouble. Luckily, the truce between the vampires and my people is shaky at best and Muncie? It's total vamp territory. Thanks to my new vamp roomie, I get a pass, and I try to forget all about the call of the wolf. It's tough, though. I... I just can't forget my embarrassment—and my anger—from that night.

And then *he* shows up and my chance at forgetting flies out the damn wind.

Ryker Wolfson. He was supposed to be my fated mate, but he chose his pack over our bond. At least, he did—but now that he knows what I've been hiding, he wants me back.

But doesn't he remember?

I told him I'll never be his mate, and there isn't a single thing he can do to change my mind.

To Ryker, that sounds like a challenge. And if there's one thing I know about wolf shifters, it's that they can never resist a challenge.

Just like I'm finding it more difficult than I should to resist *him*.

---

* ***Never His Mate*** is the first novel in the *Claw and Fang* series. It's a steamy rejected mates shifter romance, and though the hero eventually realizes his

mistake, the fierce, independent heroine isn't the sweet wolf everyone thinks she's supposed to be...

** Sarah Spade is a pen name for Jessica Lynch. If you like the *Claws Clause* series and would like to see a different spin on shifters and vampires—written in first person, and featuring fated/rejected mates—check out the *Claws and Fangs* series coming soon!

Start with Never His Mate!
Or get Gem & Ryker's complete story here.

ALSO BY SARAH SPADE

Holiday Hunk

Halloween Boo

This Christmas

Auld Lang Mine

I'm With Cupid

Getting Lucky

When Sparks Fly

Holiday Hunk: the Complete Series

Claws and Fangs

Leave Janelle

Never His Mate

Always Her Mate

Forever Mates

Hint of Her Blood

Taste of His Skin

Stay With Me

Never Say Never: Gem & Ryker

Sombra Demons

Sunglasses at Night

Ain't No Angel

True Angel

Ghost of Jealousy

Night Angel

Broken Wings

Of Santa and Slaying

Lost Angel

Born to Run

Uptown Girl

A Pack of Lies

Here Kitty, Kitty

Ordinance 7304: the Bond Laws (Claws Clause Collection #1)

Living on a Prayer (Claws Clause Collection #2)

Printed in Great Britain
by Amazon